MINECRAFT

OFFICIAL SURVIVAL STICKER BOOK

By Craig Jelley and Stephanie Milton
Designed by Joe Bolder and Paul Lang
Illustrated by Ryan Marsh
Production by Louis Harvey
Special thanks to Lydia Winters, Owen Jones,
Junkboy, Martin Johansson, and Marsh Davies

Random House 🏠 New York

Published in the United States by Random House Children's Books, a division of Penguin Random House LLC, 1745 Broadway,
New York, NY 10019, and in Canada by Penguin Random House Canada Limited, Toronto. Random House and the colophon are registered
trademarks of Penguin Random House LLC. Originally published in the United Kingdom by Egmont Publishing UK, London, in 2017.
rhcbooks.com
minecraft.net
ISBN 978-0-593-12278-5
MANUFACTURED IN CHINA
10 9 8 7 6 5 4 3 2 1
2019 Random House Children's Books Edition

NICE TO MEET YOU!

Oh, hi! I just love making new friends! Before you begin your journey into the wonderful world of Minecraft, let's have a little bit of fun with your appearance.

Choose stickers to create your character, then you can head off on your very first adventure!

BASIC CRAFTING

You must be prepared for danger at all times. Nowhere is safe!

You'll need wood to survive. Collect stickers to craft wood planks, sticks, and most importantly, a crafting table.

WOOD PLANKS RECIPE

4

CRAFTING TABLE RECIPE

STICKS RECIPE

4

TOOLS AND WEAPONS

Keep an eye on your surroundings when you're out and about—you can find all the materials you need to craft an inventory full of tools and weapons.

Read the clue underneath each recipe, then find the correct tool sticker to fill the output slot.

Mobs of the Minecraft world, beware—you've just crafted your first weapon! It can be swung quickly at hostile enemies, and makes light work of obstacles like cobwebs.

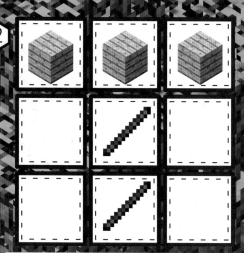

The most important tool for collecting resources, you might want to pack two or three of these before you go mining. It can break through stone and coal ore with ease.

4

③

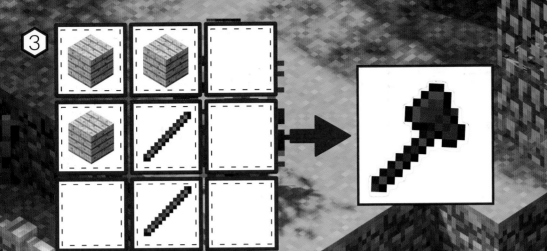

No longer will you have to punch trees to collect wood. This handy tool will chop through trees in no time. It can also be used to battle mobs, although it's a bit slower than specialized weapons.

④

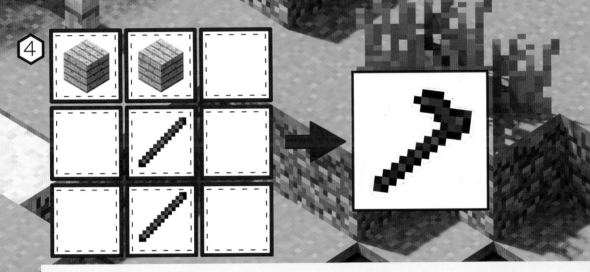

For the nature-loving player, this tool will allow you to turn dirt and grass into farmland so you can plant seeds, grow crops, and nurture flowers.

⑤

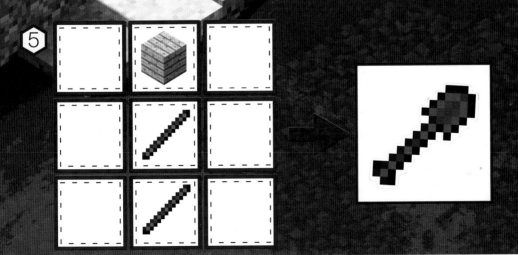

This handy item is best used to dig out and collect blocks like dirt, sand, and clay. Just remember the number one rule when using this item—never dig straight down.

MOB ENTHUSIAST

The mobs you see roaming the land around you are simply fascinating! And they're rather friendly . . . well, most of them. They're also an excellent source of items, many of which are really quite tasty.

Find the stickers on your sticker sheet to complete each of the info cards.

DID YOU KNOW?

Mob is short for "mobile," which means any living, moving creature in Minecraft. That includes friendly animals and villagers, as well as not-so-friendly monsters, and they all behave in different ways.

COW

Hostility	0	Health	10
Attack	0	XP	3
Drops			

ℹ Cows will follow you around within 10 blocks if you're holding wheat.

BAT

Hostility	0	Health	6
Attack	0	XP	0
Drops		Nothing	

ℹ Bats will only spawn in caves that have a light level of 3 or less.

PIG

Hostility	0	Health	10
Attack	0	XP	3
Drops			

ℹ You can place a saddle on a pig to ride it, then control it with a carrot on a stick.

CHICKEN

Hostility	0	Health	4
Attack	0	XP	3
Drops			

ℹ Adult chickens lay an egg once every 10 minutes, which can hatch a baby chick.

SHEEP

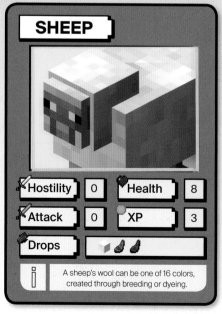

Hostility	0	Health	8
Attack	0	XP	3
Drops			

ℹ A sheep's wool can be one of 16 colors, created through breeding or dyeing.

ENDERMAN

Hostility	5	Health	40
Attack	3	XP	5
Drops			

ℹ Endermen will turn hostile to any player who makes eye contact with them.

POLAR BEAR

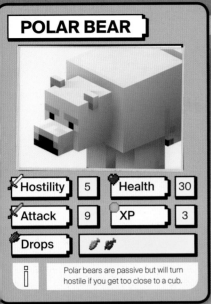

Hostility	5	Health	30
Attack	9	XP	3
Drops			

Polar bears are passive but will turn hostile if you get too close to a cub.

MOOSHROOM

Hostility	0	Health	10
Attack	0	XP	3
Drops			

If you shear a mooshroom, it will drop red mushrooms and turn into a cow!

PARROT

Hostility	0	Health	6
Attack	0	XP	3
Drops			

When tamed, parrots will follow you around or even sit on your shoulders!

RABBIT

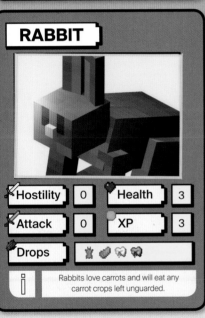

Hostility	0	Health	3
Attack	0	XP	3
Drops			

Rabbits love carrots and will eat any carrot crops left unguarded.

HORSE

Hostility	0	Health	15
Attack	0	XP	3
Drops			

Horses can equip special armor made from leather, iron, gold, or diamond!

WOLF

Hostility	5	Health	8
Attack	6	XP	3
Drops	Nothing		

Wolves won't get food poisoning from eating raw chicken or rotten flesh.

SQUID

Hostility	0	Health	10
Attack	0	XP	3
Drops			

Squid are a source of ink sacs, an item used to dye items black.

OCELOT

Hostility	0	Health	10
Attack	0	XP	3
Drops	Nothing		

An ocelot is the only thing that will scare away the explosive creeper.

LLAMA

Hostility	0	Health	30
Attack	0	XP	3
Drops			

Llamas can carry chests with them to create a moveable storage unit.

TREASURE HUNTER

You stumble across a mineshaft and head inside to hunt for treasure, but you quickly get lost. In a situation like this, it's important not to panic.

Find a route through the mine to the exit, collecting resources and avoiding hostile mobs along the way.

LAPIS LAZULI ORE

REDSTONE ORE

START

DIAMOND ORE

OU 2369

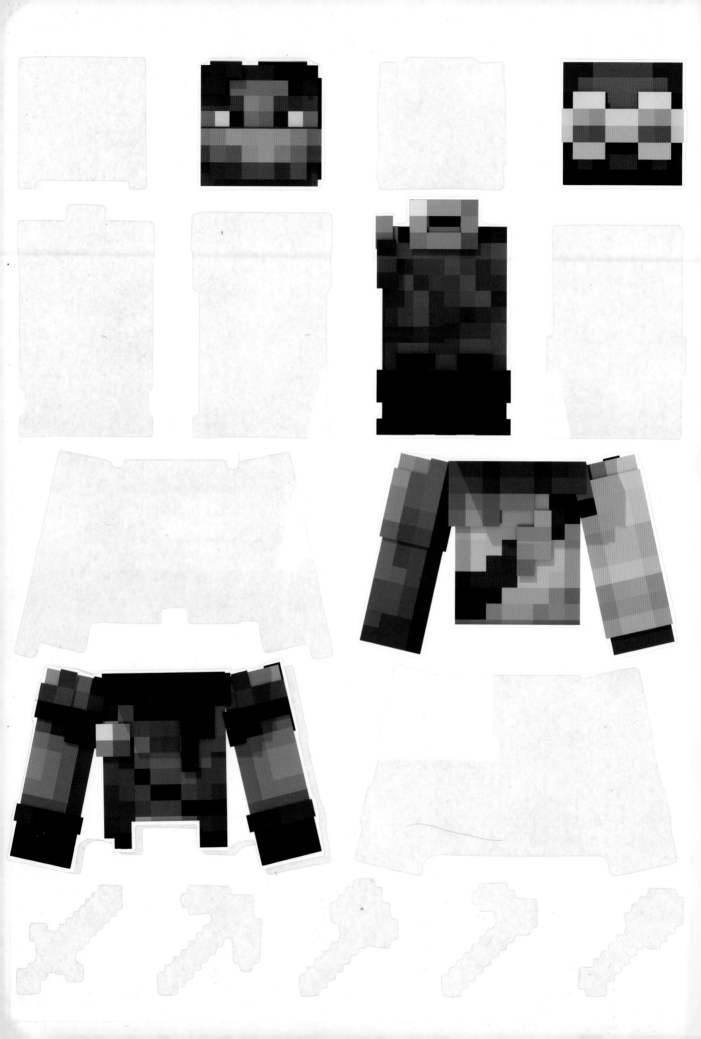

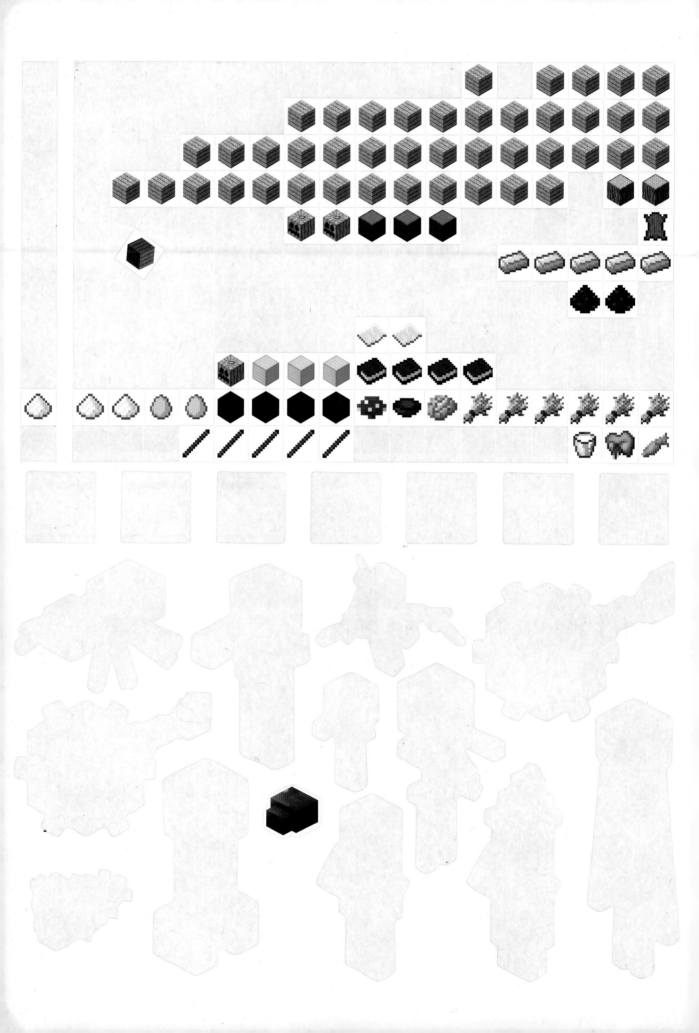

IRON ORE

COAL ORE

EMERAL

GOLD ORE

TAKING SHELTER

The sun is setting, so it's time to make a basic shelter.
Oh, good—I just love building!

Complete the crafting grids, then add each of your new
items to this abandoned cave to turn it into a home.

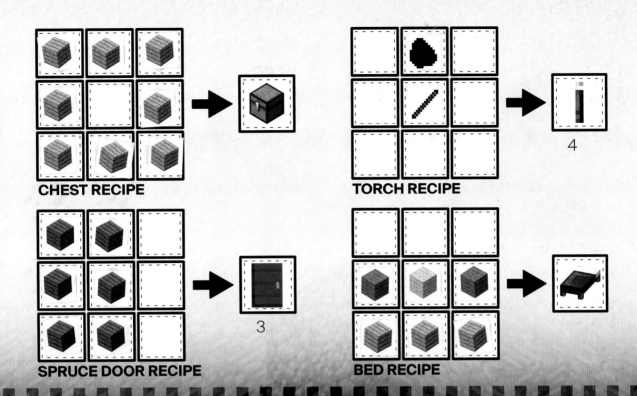

CHEST RECIPE

TORCH RECIPE

4

SPRUCE DOOR RECIPE

3

BED RECIPE

NIGHTTIME TERROR

Night is here. You climb into bed, but terrifying sounds fill the air and you can't sleep. Are you ready for your first hostile mob encounter?

Use the stickers from your sticker sheet to complete the story of your first night in Minecraft.

Suddenly, there's a knock on the . You leap out of

bed and grab a from your inventory.

You see a hole in the wall and peek through. There's a

 lurking right outside. There's a bang on the door—

something else is out there! You throw open the door,

 in hand, and a ferocious  charges in.

You panic and run outside, trapping the mob inside the

shelter. You realize you've made a mistake. The whole

area is flooded with s. You throw a in

desperation, but the mobs keep coming. All of a

sudden, the sun appears over the horizon. A

disintegrates in a blaze of fire, leaving behind a .

Now there's just the trapped  to deal with. You

open the door and get ready to charge,

but the  is nowhere to be seen. . . .

TIME TO GO PRO

Congratulations! You survived the first night despite the considerable danger. Now you've got a thirst for adventure and are ready to explore, but you'll need better equipment if you expect to survive.

Complete the crafting grids and display your new armor on the armor stand.

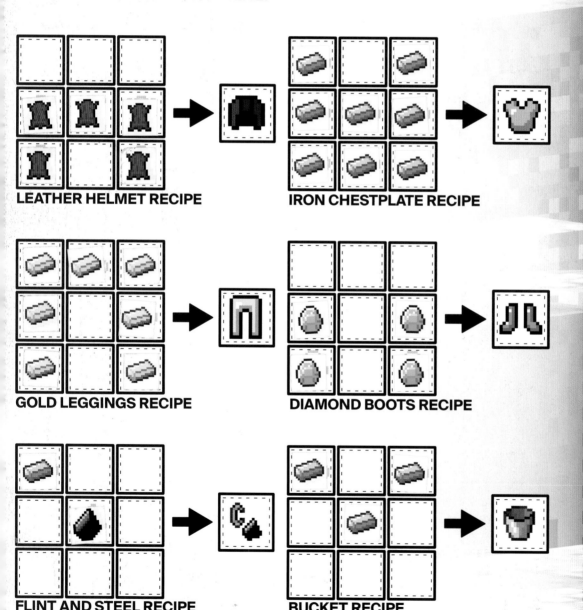

LEATHER HELMET RECIPE

IRON CHESTPLATE RECIPE

GOLD LEGGINGS RECIPE

DIAMOND BOOTS RECIPE

FLINT AND STEEL RECIPE

BUCKET RECIPE

WHERE TO NEXT?

The ocean is no obstacle for a keen explorer like you. With compass in hand, you set sail for one of the strange new biomes you can see in the distance. Wonderful discoveries await you!

Find the biome sticker to fill each space, then follow the instructions on page 17 to find a path to your next destination.

EXTREME HILLS

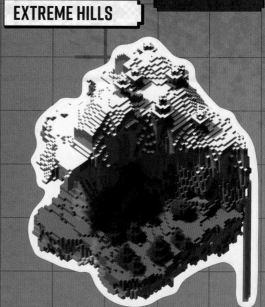

MESA

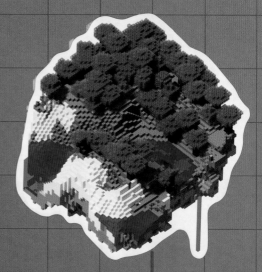

ROOFED FOREST

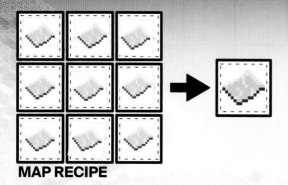

MAP RECIPE

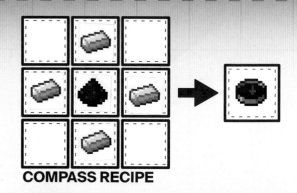

COMPASS RECIPE

16

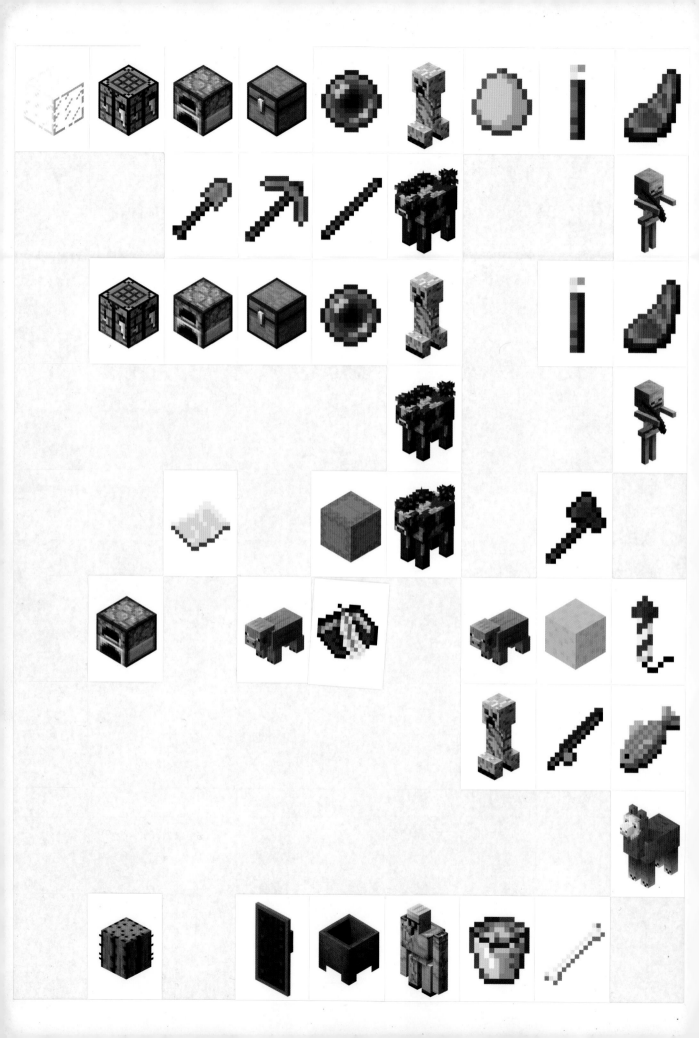

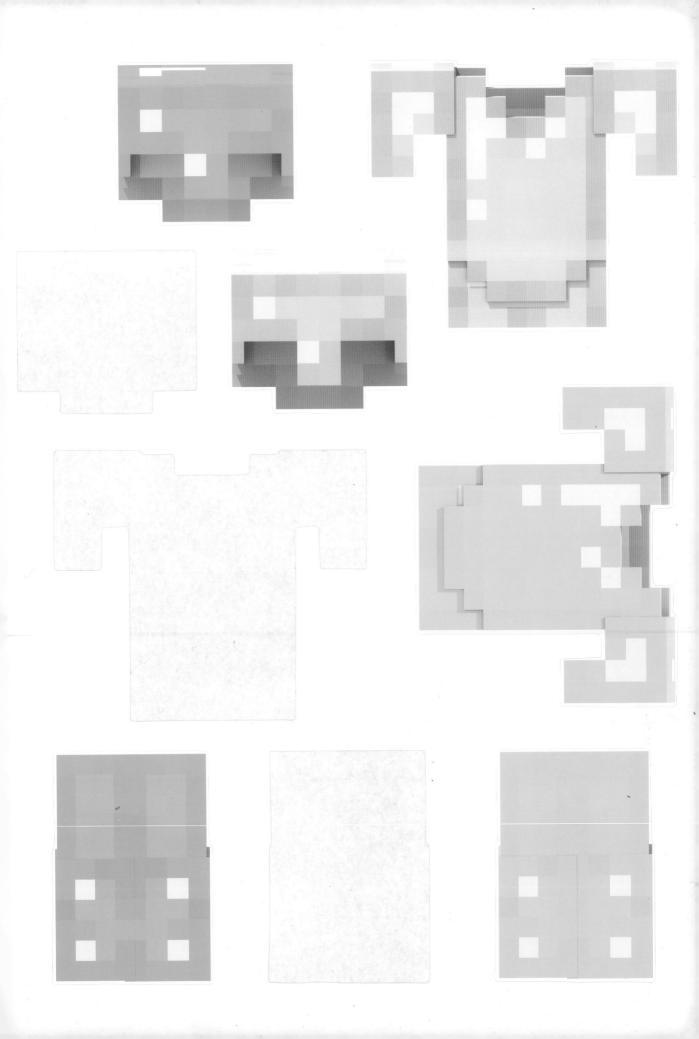

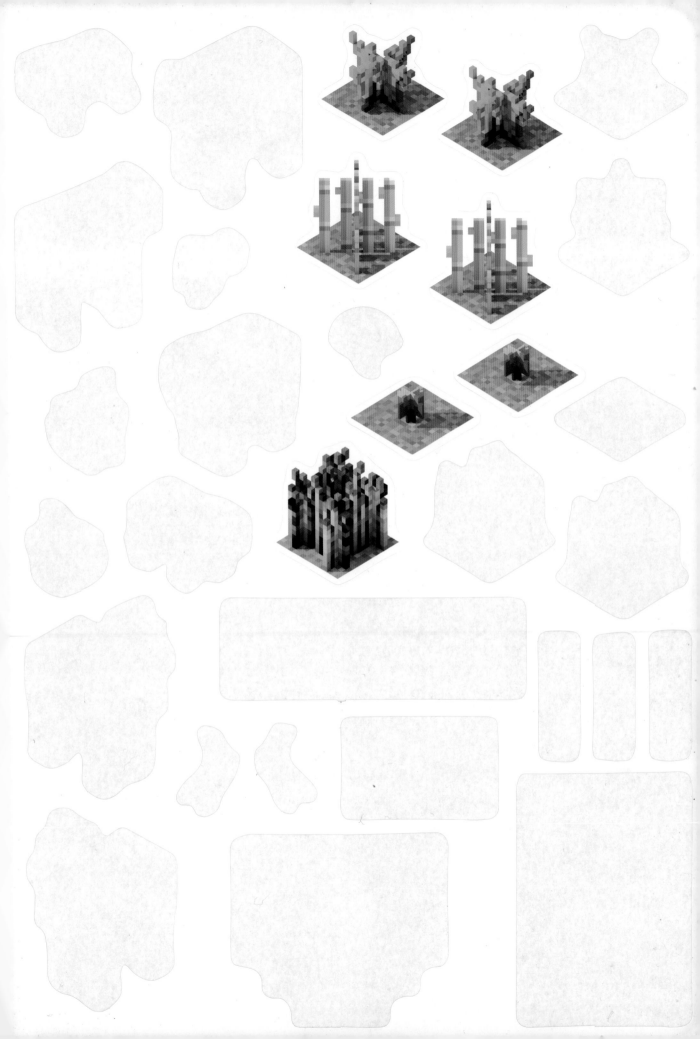

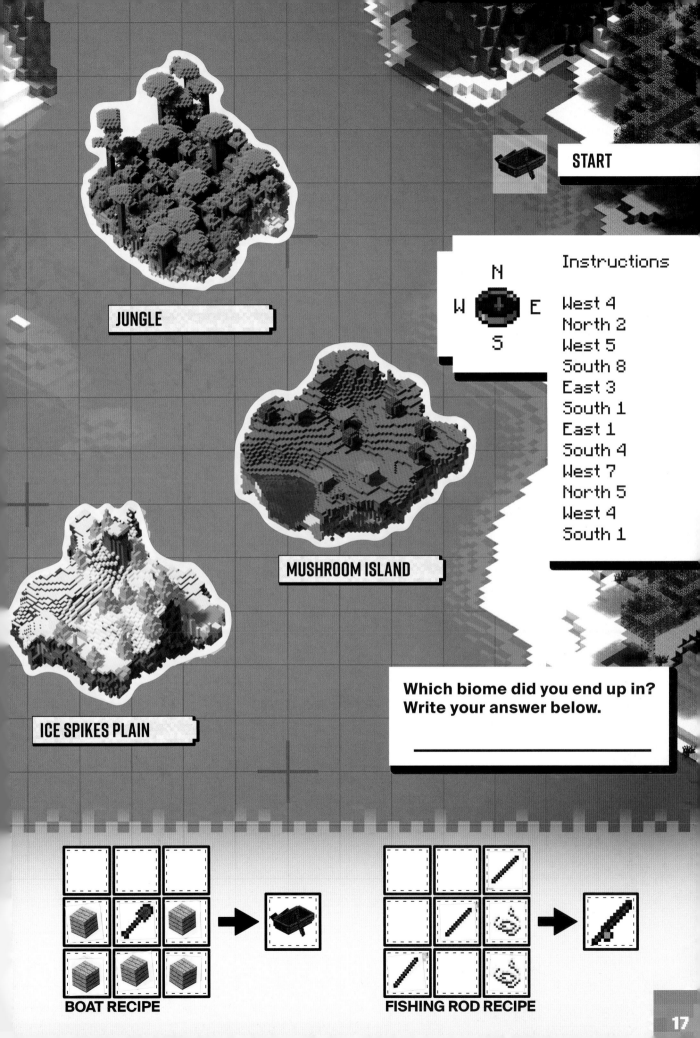

START

JUNGLE

Instructions

West 4
North 2
West 5
South 8
East 3
South 1
East 1
South 4
West 7
North 5
West 4
South 1

MUSHROOM ISLAND

ICE SPIKES PLAIN

Which biome did you end up in? Write your answer below.

_____

BOAT RECIPE

FISHING ROD RECIPE

MAPPING YOUR WORLD

Maps are wonderful items. They allow you to mark the locations of the sights you see on your travels so you can find them again.

Place the naturally generated structure stickers in the correct spaces to learn more about them.

IGLOO

Igloos are small structures found in ice plains biomes. They contain several useful items and sometimes loot.

WOODLAND MANSION

A rare sight in roofed forest biomes, woodland mansions are packed with resources and hostile mobs.

WITCH HUT

Witch huts can be spotted in swamp biomes. Each hut is home to a witch and contains brewing equipment.

DUNGEON

These small rooms can be found underground. They contain a monster spawner and loot chests.

STRONGHOLD

You'll need to find an underground stronghold if you want to visit the End. Throw eyes of ender to locate them.

ABANDONED MINESHAFT

Hidden underground, abandoned mineshafts are a great place to mine for ores and search for loot.

VILLAGE

You'll find friendly villagers to trade with in desert, plains, savanna, and taiga biomes.

DESERT TEMPLE

Desert temples are found in desert biomes. There's a hidden chamber underneath the main floor.

MONSTER HUNTER

If you're looking for advice on how to deal with Minecraft's most dangerous mobs, you've come to the right person. I was born for this!

Find the stickers on your sticker sheets to complete each of the mob cards and learn more about these dangerous monsters.

SPIDER

Hostility	5	Health	16
Attack	3	XP	3
Drops			

Unlike most mobs, spiders are able to climb up and over tall walls.

GUARDIAN

Hostility	9	Health	30
Attack	9	XP	10
Drops			

Guardians cause damage with their spikes when a player attacks them.

ELDER GUARDIAN

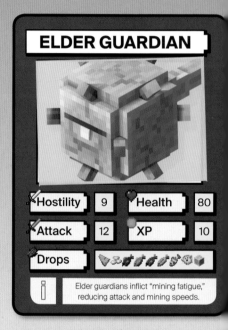

Hostility	9	Health	80
Attack	12	XP	10
Drops			

Elder guardians inflict "mining fatigue," reducing attack and mining speeds.

SILVERFISH

Hostility	6	Health	8
Attack	1	XP	5
Drops		Nothing	

Silverfish are so small that they'll sink into soul sand and suffocate.

WITCH

Hostility	8	Health	26
Attack	6	XP	5
Drops			

Witches cause damage by throwing a variety of splash potions.

VINDICATOR

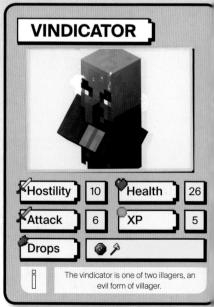

Hostility	10	Health	26
Attack	6	XP	5
Drops			

The vindicator is one of two illagers, an evil form of villager.

EVOKER

Hostility	10	Health	24
Attack	6	XP	10
Drops			

This illager mob is capable of summoning swarms of vex.

VEX

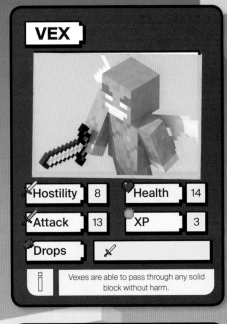

Hostility	8	Health	14
Attack	13	XP	3
Drops			

Vexes are able to pass through any solid block without harm.

ZOMBIE

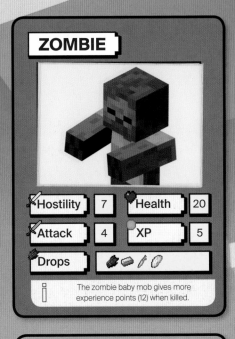

Hostility	7	Health	20
Attack	4	XP	5
Drops			

The zombie baby mob gives more experience points (12) when killed.

CREEPER

Hostility	8	Health	20
Attack	49	XP	5
Drops			

Creepers are an explosive menace and become charged when hit by lightning.

SKELETON

Hostility	7	Health	20
Attack	5	XP	5
Drops			

The skeleton can be seen all over the Overworld and in Nether fortresses.

ENDERMITE

Hostility	6	Health	6
Attack	3	XP	3
Drops		Nothing	

Minecraft's smallest mob occasionally spawns when an ender pearl is thrown.

SLIME

Hostility	7	Health	16
Attack	4	XP	4
Drops			

There are three sizes of slime. Only the tiny ones drop slimeballs.

STRAY

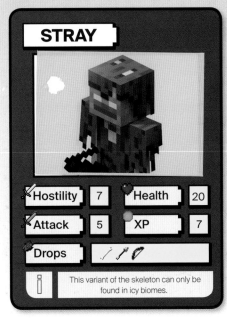

Hostility	7	Health	20
Attack	5	XP	7
Drops			

This variant of the skeleton can only be found in icy biomes.

HUSK

Hostility	7	Health	20
Attack	4	XP	7
Drops			

The husk is a variant of zombie found in desert biomes.

ENCHANTER

A survival expert is always learning new skills. The time has come to set up an enchantment room so you can make improvements to your equipment.

Use the code below to unlock the secrets of the enchantment books' strange language.

1

— — — — —

2

— — — —

3

— — — — — — — —

4

— — — — —

5

— — — — — — — — —

6

— — — —

CODE

∧	∧	∧	⌐	⌐	⌐L	=	⌐	=	⌐	¦	⊦	⊦	⌐J	⌐ノ	>	¦⌐	⌐ら
A	B	C	D	E	F	G	H	I	J	K	L	M	N	O	P	Q

7

‗ ‗ ‗ ‗ ‗ ‗ ‗

8

‗ ‗ ‗ ‗ ‗ ‗ ‗

9

‗ ‗ ‗ ‗ ‗ ‗

R   S   T   U   V   W   X   Y   Z

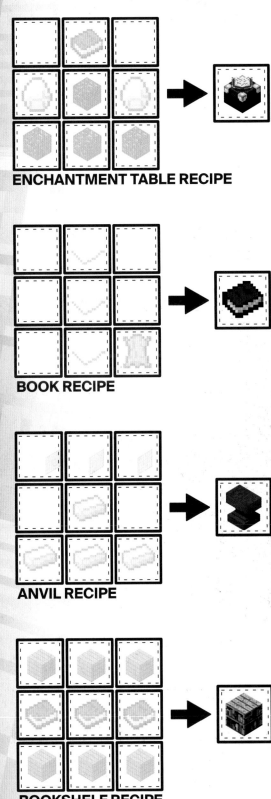

ENCHANTMENT TABLE RECIPE

BOOK RECIPE

ANVIL RECIPE

BOOKSHELF RECIPE

FARMING AND BAKING

I don't know about you, but exploring makes me hungry. Luckily you've collected lots of crops and animals on your travels—enough to start your own farm, in fact.

Complete the recipes and fill the outdoor space with crops and friendly mobs.

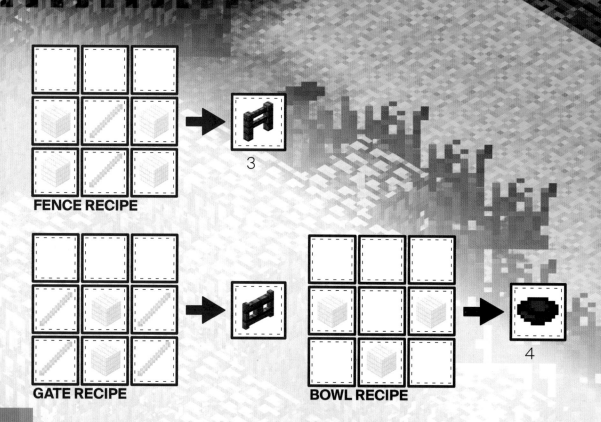

FENCE RECIPE

GATE RECIPE

BOWL RECIPE

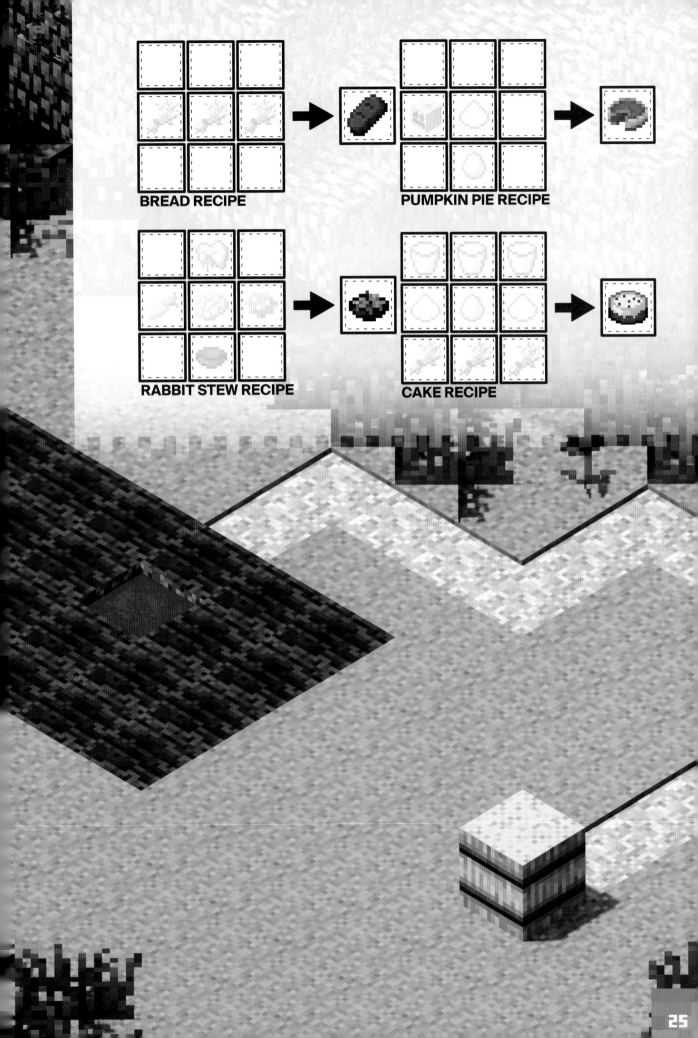

BREAD RECIPE

PUMPKIN PIE RECIPE

RABBIT STEW RECIPE

CAKE RECIPE

HIDDEN DANGER

You've spotted a small village full of friendly villagers. This could be your chance to make some friends, but a dangerous situation arises. . . .

Use the stickers from your sticker sheet to fill in the gaps and create your own story.

As you enter the village, you see a shop with a

 outside. You approach the building and

a  appears from nowhere. "Hello!" you shout

excitedly. The stares at you blankly, then makes

some funny sounds. You don't know what it's saying,

but a range of items are now displayed before you,

including a and a . You reach out to

touch one of the items but accidentally attack instead.

The jumps back in horror and runs away.

The village is in a panic, and all of a sudden, several

enormous  approach you. You swing your

 and defeat one of them instantly. It topples

over and disappears, dropping a . You pick up

the treasure and run away from the village as fast as

you can. That did not go well!

MINECART RAILWAY

Wouldn't it be fun to visit your lovely new friends by minecart next time? It's definitely the best way to travel!

Fill the gaps with rail stickers to complete the track from your base to the village.

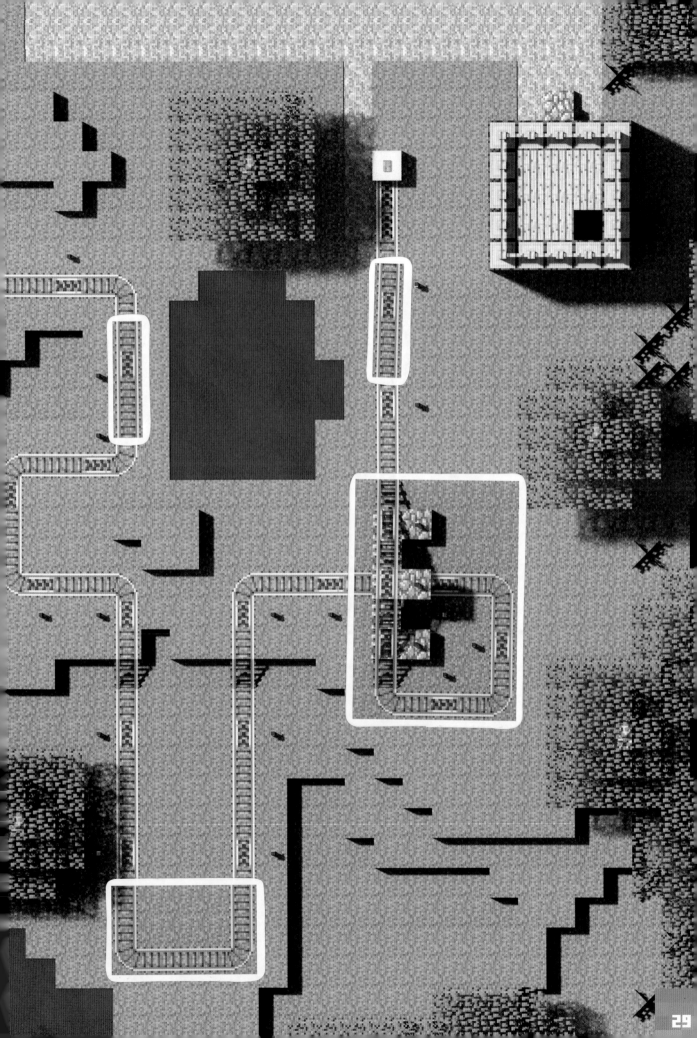

MASTER BUILDER

Gosh, look at all the amazing loot you've collected on your travels! Oh, good—that means we can build something new! I just love building!

Let your creative side loose and create an amazing new base with any blocks you want!

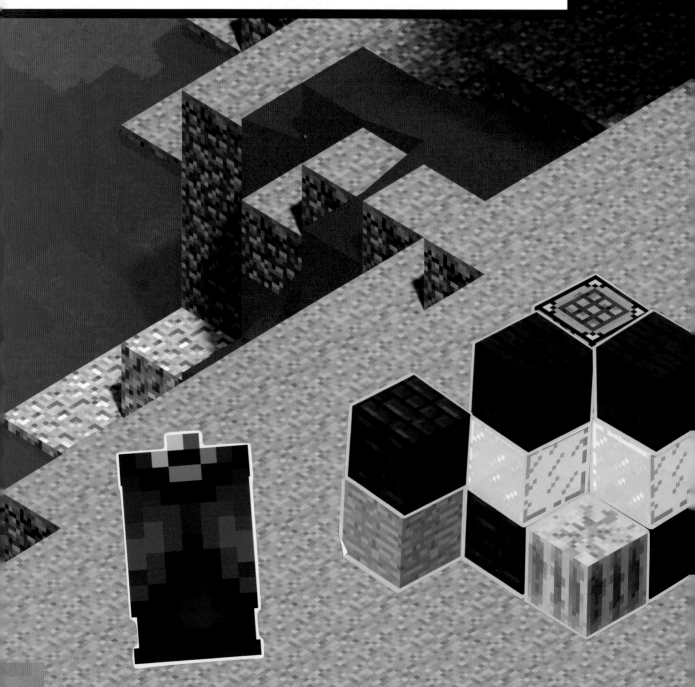

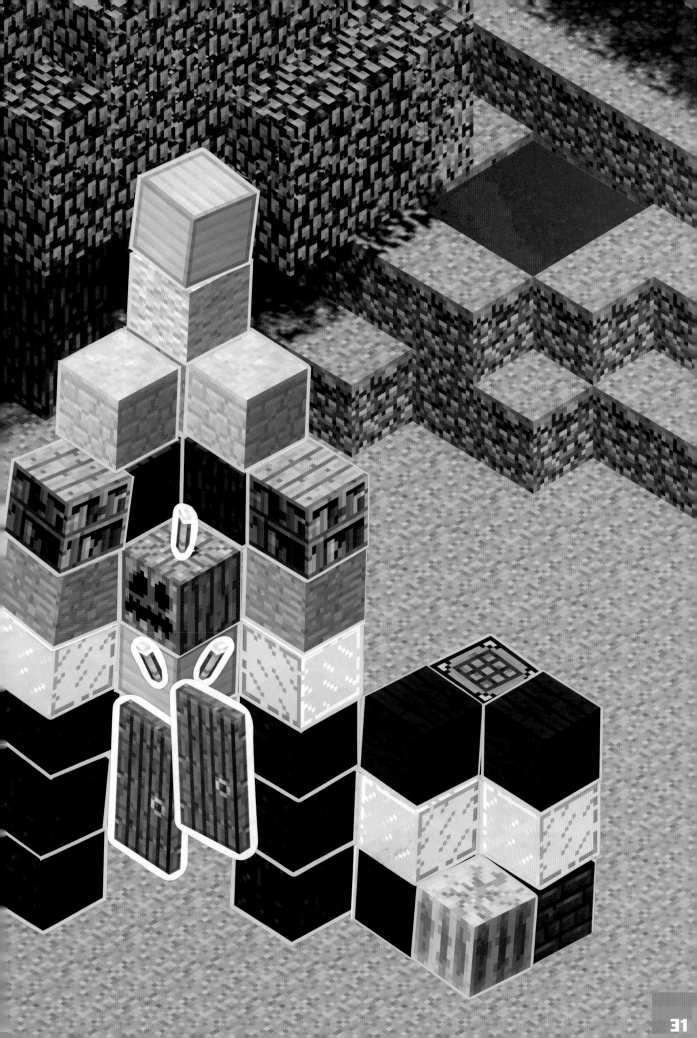

SECURITY GUARD

Before you can relax and enjoy your new home, make sure it's properly defended. You must always be prepared for danger!

Find and place the iron golem sticker beside the snow golem, so they can protect your base while you take a well-earned break.

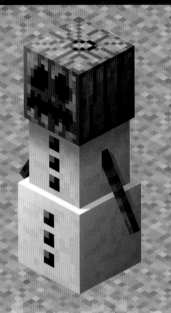

ANSWERS

Pages 4–5:
1. Sword
2. Pickaxe
3. Ax
4. Hoe
5. Shovel

Pages 8–9:

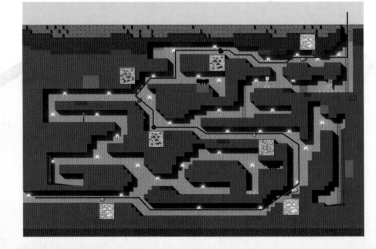

Pages 16–17:
Roofed Forest

Pages 22–23:
1. Water
2. Grow
3. Humanoid
4. Twist
5. Elemental
6. Fire
7. Animal
8. Sphere
9. Beast

YOU'RE THE DETECTIVE!

You're The Detective!

24 Solve-Them-Yourself Picture Mysteries

Lawrence Treat

ILLUSTRATED BY KATHLEEN BOROWIK

DAVID R. GODINE · PUBLISHER · BOSTON

First published in 1983 by
David R. Godine, *Publisher*
Post Office Box 450
Jaffrey, New Hampshire 03452
www.godine.com

Library of Congress Catalog Card No.: 82-49346

ISBN: 0-87923-478-4

Design by Hal Morgan
Cover art by Leslie Cabarga

Seventh printing, 2004
Manufactured in Canada

CONTENTS

Confidential!   7

Bomb Sight   10

Watch Out!   12

Made in Japan   14

Buried Gold   16

Stolen Bases   18

Picnic   20

Piggy Bank   22

Blot It Out   24

Seeing Double   26

International Crisis   28

Picture Gallery   30

The Cheater   32

The Cider Booth   34

Gambol   36

Cookie Jar   38

Water Bed   40

False Alarm   42

Westward Ho-Hum!   44

Trick or Treat   46

Spelling Bee   48

The Great Diamond Heist   50

The Gentle Breezes   52

Idora Park   54

The Big Bang   56

Solutions   59

What the Young Detective Ought to Know   75

Dear Reader,

First of all, you ought to know how I made these puzzles. They depend on the clues in the pictures, and there are three kinds of clues. There are the pictures in which some object is missing, like a rowboat with no oars. Next, there are the ones with a broken object, like a rowboat with broken oars. And third, there are the ones with an object that shouldn't be there, like the same rowboat with nobody in it except a kangaroo, which everybody knows comes from Australia and can't swim. At least I don't think it can, but if I'm wrong, write me and tell me so.

Once you spot one of these three types of clues, you've made a good start. Sometimes the clue solves the puzzle all by itself, but at other times it's just the first step. For instance, in the case of the kangaroo in the rowboat, you start by asking yourself how to get hold of a kangaroo. If the text says that one of the suspects works in a factory that makes the holes in button-holes and another one works in a zoo, you can be pretty sure that the zookeeper is the man you're after.

Sometimes the text gives you important facts, and usually the answers to the questions help you find the solution.

There are lots of possibilities, but the best way to handle these cases is to look at the picture, then read the text and the questions, maybe without even trying to answer them at first. After that, look at the picture again, study it carefully, and read the text a second time. The clue might be in the picture or in the text, or it might be a simple matter of common knowledge, such as the fact that you can't row a boat if you have no oars.

Remember that you work on probabilities, just like the police do in real-life cases. In arithmetic there's only one answer and you're sure of it, but in criminal cases there are often several possibilities, and you have to reason things out and hope that you're right.

Suppose, for instance, that someone says that Ruthie Picklewish broke the window of a house and stole a twenty dollar bill that was lying on a table. If there's blood on the window and Ruthie has a cut on her hand, you'd have reason enough to accuse her. Nevertheless, it's quite possible that Ruthie happened to be near the house when the thief accidentally dropped the bill and that Ruthie picked it up, and that she cut her hand earlier in the day, while scraping carrots. So—which theory is more likely? It's up to you.

And don't worry if you can't solve all the puzzles. Even Whiz McGonnigle, whom you'll meet while reading the book, couldn't solve them all, and he's been detecting ever since he was a baby and solved the mystery of his missing pacifier. So if you get stuck on a puzzle, try moving on to the next one and coming back to the sticky one later on. Whiz, who has a sense of humor, advises standing on your head for a while to clear your brain. And if you can't stand on your head, stand on your feet. That's easier.

These puzzles, then, are a game of observation and of logic, but mostly, this book is fun. It was fun to write, and I think it will be fun to solve these cases. Some of them are easy, but I tried to make some of them very, very hard to give you a good challenge.

Good luck!

Lawrence Treat

You're the Detective!

BOMB SIGHT

M**r.** Bumbledee, a teacher, was in the main office of the Pilgrim Hat Elementary School when the phone rang. The principal answered, listened for a moment, then stammered into the phone. His face was white and his voice shook, and he dropped the receiver.

"There's a bomb in the broom closet," he said, "and it's going to explode as soon as it's touched, or maybe sooner."

"Then ring the fire alarm and get everybody out of school," said Mr. Bumbledee.

The principal disagreed. "No, because that means that everybody on the second floor has to walk right past the closet where the bomb is. The kids are much safer where they are. I'll call the fire department and see what they say."

"There may not be time for that," Mr. Bumbledee said. "I don't know what to do."

"Go look," the principal said.

Trembling, Mr. Bumbledee tiptoed upstairs to the closet and carefully opened the door. He kept staring at the wires but he was afraid to touch them. Then he became aware that somebody else was looking at the bomb, too. Turning around, Mr. Bumbledee saw a small, intent boy wearing glasses.

"Get away from here," Mr. Bumbledee said. "The thing might explode."

The small boy was Whiz McGonnigle. What do you think he said?

Questions

1. Does the mechanism in the closet contain the essential parts of a bomb? Yes_____ No_____

2. Is it dangerous to touch a live bomb? Yes_____ No_____

3. Was the clock mechanism designed to set off the bomb? Yes_____ No_____

4. Could you render the bomb harmless by disconnecting the wires? Yes_____ No_____

5. Can you trace the wires with a pencil or your finger? Yes_____ No_____

6. What does this tell you about the bomb?

7. What do you think Whiz said?

Solution on page 59

WATCH OUT!

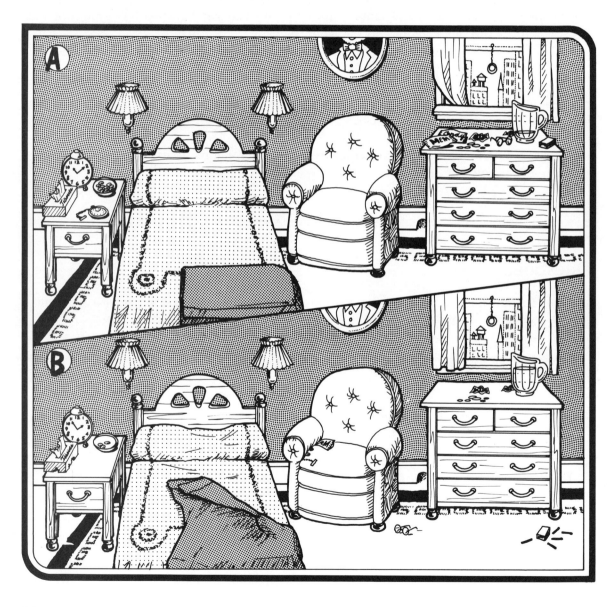

Mr. Bigbelly Bewilliger couldn't cook, so he lived in a hotel, and since hotel meals are expensive, he ate a lot of junk candy. Naturally, his teeth suffered, with the result that one of them had to be pulled. But on the day of his appointment with the dentist he chickened out and went to sleep instead.

Sketch A shows Mr. Bewilliger's hotel room before he took his nap, and B shows it when he woke up and discovered—to his horror—that his watch was missing from his bedside table.

Can you decide why the watch was missing from the table and what Mr. Bewilliger should do about it?

Questions

1. List at least ten differences between A and B.

2. Do you think that the maid came into the room while Mr. Bewilliger was asleep? Yes_____ No_____ No evidence_____

3. Do you think that a thief came into the room while Mr. Bewilliger was asleep? Yes_____ No_____ No evidence_____

4. Who moved the watch?

Solution on page 59

MADE IN JAPAN

On her tenth birthday Jenny Jackalanda invited seven of her friends, James, Jack, Joseph, Jerry, Jane, Jacqueline, and Jill, to a party. They all came and sat down at a table that had a huge decorated birthday cake in the middle. And there was a small green horse on a little platform in the center of the cake.

"It's made out of jade," Jenny said. "It's called a *netsuke*"—which she pronounced "net'su kē"—"and it's terribly valuable. The Japanese used to put it on the string that they fastened their kimonos with, because the kimonos had no buttons. My uncle lived in Japan and he gave it to me for my birthday. Isn't it cute?"

Jenny's friends agreed, but secretly they thought that she was bragging and that she'd put the netsuke in the center of the cake so that nobody could touch it. They were too polite, however, to say anything except, "Oh, it's nice."

When it was time to blow out the candles on the cake, Jenny turned off all the lights, stood up on a chair, and took a deep breath. Then she blew, but she blew so hard that she blew over one of the candles. It fell on a paper napkin, which promptly caught fire and made everyone scramble around looking for water.

After the fire had been put out and the lights were turned back on, Jenny let out a scream. "My netsuke!" she yelled. "My birthday present! Somebody took it!"

Who?

Questions

1. Where had Jenny been sitting?

2. How was the fire put out?

3. Did the children leave their places in a hurry?

4. Why didn't anyone see who took the netsuke?

5. Did the thief leave any clues?

6. In which chair had the thief been sitting?

7. Who took the netsuke?

Solution on page 60

BURIED GOLD

The Wallamilletti family (they got that name long ago, when Wally Walla married Milly Milletti and she loved her name too much to give it up) used to talk about old man Angus Wallamilletti who died in 1918. He collected gold coins, but nobody ever found them. The family thought that he'd buried them, although nobody knew just where.

Young Wendy Wallamilletti liked to read and liked to find out things. In fact, she had read almost every book in the house except a big, heavy one with the title, *Report of State Botanist, State of New York, 1895.*

One rainy day when that was the only book left to read, Wendy opened it. It was hard reading, but when she turned the first few pages, a piece of paper fell out and Wendy became suspicious. She remembered that Angus Wallamilletti was supposed to have told his grandson, Androcles, where the gold coins were, but Androcles had been killed by a lion many years ago and therefore had never found the gold. Nor had anyone else.

Wendy studied the paper, which is reproduced here. If you were Wendy, could you find the gold?

Questions

1. Do you think that the paper contained instructions in code for how or where to find the gold? Yes_____ No_____

2. Can you rearrange the groups of letters so that they make words? Yes_____ No_____ (Suppose a friend of yours left a secret message for you that said NOPEH EM. Wouldn't you manage to rearrange the letters so that they read PHONE ME?)

3. What is the deciphered message?

4. Where would you expect to find the gold?

Solution on page 61

STOLEN BASES

The Shmozzlolers (they are the people who inhabit Shmozzloland) are wonderful athletes, but they never played baseball until the Right Honorable Igno Mwzxr (whose name nobody can pronounce, so don't even try) went to the United States to negotiate a trade treaty. Before he went to Washington, a friend took him to a ball game. He got so excited about it that he forgot all about the treaty (it never did get signed), and instead he bought a gross (144) of baseballs, some gloves and bats, three bags, and a home plate, which he set up in Shmozzloland. He forgot, however, to buy a rule book.

This sketch shows one of the early games played at Coconoco Field, in Shmozzloland. Whiz McGonnigle found ten things wrong in this picture. How many can *you* find? What are they?

Solution on page 61

PICNIC

Every morning the Fancy family chauffeur brought Gwendolyn to school, and every evening he called for her in one of the Fancy limousines (usually the red one), and every week she wore a new dress (usually a red one). She showed it off and told her classmates how rich she was.

When the class decided to have a picnic on Dead Pirate's Beach, and to swim and roast marshmallows, Gwendolyn surprised everybody by saying that she'd love to go. The chauffeur brought her to the beach and immediately took a shine to the teacher. Meanwhile Gwendolyn told her classmates that it was her birthday and that she'd been given a watch worth a thousand dollars. She showed it off and made everybody admire it, and she kept saying how expensive it was.

Gwendolyn went for a swim with the others, but when she returned to the beach her watch was gone. She cried and cried and said she *knew* that she'd put the watch down carefully with her possessions before she went in the water.

The chauffeur called the police, who searched everywhere and talked to everybody, but couldn't find the watch. Nevertheless Whiz McGonnigle, who like everybody else had no love for Gwendolyn, was pretty sure he could have found the watch, but he kept mum.

Where do you think he would have looked?

Questions

1. Are Gwendolyn's things the ones with the picnic basket and other beach items? Yes_____ No_____

2. Are expensive watches usually thin? Yes_____ No_____

3. Is a thin watch easy to conceal? Yes_____ No_____

4. Would the watch gleam in the sunlight? Yes_____ No_____

5. Do you think someone took the watch without being seen? Yes_____ No_____

6. Do you think that Gwendolyn lost the watch in the water, and then made up the theft story? Yes_____ No_____

7. Where do you think Whiz thought he could have found the watch?

Solution on page 61

PIGGY BANK

The man whom the newspapers called Hard-Hearted Hardy specialized in stealing piggy banks, which he often took in plain sight because he thought that children were not only weak and defenseless, but also too stupid to be able to identify him. He usually went into a playroom, and if any children were there, he threatened them and often knocked them down. Then, with a growl like a bear, he smashed the piggy bank and helped himself to the contents.

He got away with it for almost a year, but one day he walked into a room where Whiz McGonnigle and three of his friends were playing. When Hardy growled, they knew who he was, but instead of being scared, they jumped on him. Whiz grabbed his legs so that he fell, and the other three boys bit him as hard as they could. Nevertheless, he escaped and took the piggy bank with him. After that, he disappeared for a while. But only for a while.

On the basis of descriptions from Whiz and his friends, a police artist drew a sketch of Hardy. The boys agreed that it was excellent in every detail, but the picture was of limited use until the police had a suspect, and at first they had none.

Four months later, however, the police arrested three men because they were spending large sums of money in small change. The sketches of the three are labeled A, B, and C. One of them was probably Hard-Hearted Hardy, although well disguised. Nevertheless, after comparing the three sketches with the original one of Hardy, Whiz and his friends were able to point out which of the three had robbed them.

Can you?

Questions

1. Do you think it likely that Hardy disguised himself after the incident with the four boys? Yes____ No____

2. Is a beard a likely disguise? Yes____ No____

3. Is a mustache a likely disguise? Yes____ No____

4. Does a different type of haircut change the appearance of a person? Yes____ No____

5. Is it possible that Hardy underwent plastic surgery after the incident with the four boys? Yes____ No____

6. Whose nose most resembles Hardy's?_____

7. Whose mouth most resembles Hardy's?_____

8. Whose ears most closely resemble Hardy's?_____

9. Which sketch is Hardy? A____ B____ C____

Solution on page 62

23

BLOT IT OUT

Whiz McGonnigle knew he shouldn't have done it, but he did it anyway.

He was spending Wednesday afternoon with his friend, Skinny Hobart, when Skinny suggested going up to the attic to see what they could find. That was all right, but when they passed the cook's room on the third floor and the door was open, Whiz said, "Let's go in."

The cook's name was Cheri, which the two boys thought was funny. Whiz, who was always looking into things, looked into Cheri's open desk and saw an inkwell and an old-fashioned pen, which he took out to examine. He remembered his grandmother saying what a nuisance those pens had been, before ball-point pens were invented. She said the ink was always wet on the paper after you'd written, and that you dried it by pressing the paper down on a sheet of blotting paper, which left an impression of the letter, only *backwards,* on the blotting paper.

That's what Cheri had done, and she'd been using a brand-new sheet of blotting paper so you could almost read what she'd written, except that it was backwards.

Whiz picked up the blotting paper to study, but just then there was a noise, so the two boys ran out of the room and up into the attic, with Whiz still holding the blotter. A couple of minutes later they heard Cheri's voice say, "My blotter's gone. I bet it's that kid." Then a man's voice said, "I'll teach him to go snooping around. Wait till I get hold of him."

Cheri said, "I bet he's in the attic. And that blotter—if he has it—"

The man's voice said, "Don't worry. Maybe he went in, but he's not going to come out."

Whiz knew that somehow he had to read that blotter, and fast. Can you? What do you think he and Skinny Hobart should do?

Solution on page 62

SEEING DOUBLE

Martha McGonnigle thought that a chair was a chair and a mountain was a mountain, and each was the same thing for everybody. But her parents tried to explain how the world and everything in it looked different to everybody. They said that we were all individuals, and that no two individuals were exactly alike, and that therefore everyone sees things differently.

Martha didn't understand what her parents were saying, so she brought up the subject to the principal at her school, who suggested that Martha try an experiment. So Martha asked two friends to sit outside the gym door and sketch what they saw, while Martha watched them to make sure that neither one of them looked at what the other was drawing. The friends were Lily Valley, who always got A's in science; and Violet Brookside, who didn't do well in science, but was a whiz at English and history.

Of the two sketches shown here, "A" is by Lily and "B" is by Violet. They show different types of minds and different interests. For example, I once went to a movie in which there was a prairie scene where the outlaw was preparing to ambush the sheriff. I saw merely the action, but the professional bird watcher with whom I discussed the movie later asked me whether I'd noticed the Western Mockingbird. I hadn't, but to him, it was the high point of the entire movie.

What differences can you find between "A" and "B"? Why do you think each girl emphasized what she emphasized?

Solution on page 63

INTERNATIONAL CRISIS

It was hard for Martha McGonnigle to believe, but here she was in Europe, and staying at the U.S. Embassy because her father was an aide to the American representative in formulating an important international treaty. But on the day before the final get-together of the various key delegates, Martha's father almost sent her home.

"There's been a threat," he told Martha, "and if anything happens to one of us, then the whole treaty will be lost and our work will be for nothing. Which is what the terrorist wants—whoever he is."

"You mean somebody may get killed?" Martha asked.

Her father nodded and Martha said, "Including you?" Her father nodded again and Martha said, "Gee! What can you do?"

"Hope," her father said. "And maybe spot the assassin in time."

During the previous days Martha had been all over the embassy, in the kitchens and the storerooms and the records room and most of the offices. After the first day, nobody paid much attention to her. "McGonnigle's kid," they said, gave her a smile, and let her do whatever she wanted.

Consequently, on the day of the final meeting Martha had free rein to find evidence of the plot against the treaty, but about all she managed to accomplish was to make a nuisance of herself, until the hors d'oeuvres were rolled in, when...

From an examination of the sketch—what do you think Martha saw, what did she deduce, and what did she do about it?

Questions

1. Which of the following is the most likely means to use in order to kill a delegate at the embassy? A bomb_____ A gun_____ A knife_____ Poison_____

2. Would one of the delegates be a likely poisoner? Yes_____ No_____

3. Would a spy be likely to pose as a waiter? Yes_____ No_____

4. Would the waiter have a good opportunity for administering poison? Yes_____ No_____

5. Which item is best suited for containing poison?_____

6. Do you find that the contents of any of the plates arouse your suspicion? Yes_____ No_____ If yes, which plate?_____

7. Could Martha be absolutely sure which item was poisonous? Yes_____ No_____

8. What do you think Martha did?

Solution on page 64

PICTURE GALLERY

Whiz McGonnigle's mother loved picture galleries, and whenever there was a local exhibit she went several times and took Whiz with her. She had hopes that someday he'd be an artist, and although he showed talent, most people thought he'd either be a policeman or a bicycle racer. There was also a possibility that he'd become a scientist and discover a quick cure for a broken leg.

In due time the traveling exhibit of 18th and 19th-century American painters came to town and was shown at the local Whistling Gallery (they'd meant to call it the Whistler Gallery, but somebody got mixed up). Because of the importance of the show, everybody who could hold a paintbrush brought paint box and easel and sat down to copy.

Sketch A shows a section of the gallery as it was on the morning that Whiz's mother brought him to see it. He studied it with interest, but the second time he went with her, right after school was out, he got excited. "Look, Mom," he said. "Look—that one got stolen!"

What did he see?

Questions

1. Can a good artist duplicate a painting with sufficient skill to fool the average viewer? Yes____ No____ Probably____

2. Could an expert spot a good copy as against an original by looking at it on a gallery wall? Yes____ No____ Not with absolute certainty____

3. Could an expert spot a copy by close and careful study? Yes____ No____ Probably____

4. Can you tell how old a painting is by finding out the age of the canvas it's painted on? Yes____ No____ Probably____

5. Are spectrographic and X-ray analyses sure proof of the age of a painting? Yes____ No____ Probably____

6. Which painting did Whiz point out as false?

Solution on page 65

THE CHEATER

a

C. Starrs
Room 415

① In 1802, the settlers became upset because the right to set deposit at New Orleans was canceled.
② Napoleon thought he could control the U.S. by holding New Orleans, but he was never able to set up a big army there.
③ Jefferson wanted to have all of Louisiana, and buying New Orleans was the first per step in plan.
... purchase documents were signed ... May, 1803. We paid $18.00 ... 000. In French money that was ... 80 million francs.
⑤ The Federalists objected to the treaty.

Answers to a test about the Louisiana Purchase

b

U. Betcher
Room 415

1. In 1802, the settlers became upset beca use the right to deposit at New Orleans was canceled.
2. Napoleon thought he could control the U.S. by ho lding New Orleans, but he was never able to set up a big army there.
... Jefferson wanted to have all of ... ana, and buy ing New ... as was the first step ... plans.
... ree docu ments were signed ... 03. We paid ... 5,000,000. In French money ... as 80 mil lion franks.
5. The Feduriliots objictid to the treetie.

When Mr. Newman, the new fifth-grade teacher, picked up the papers that his students had piled on the corner of his desk as they finished the exam and left the room, he had no time to look at them. When he examined them later, he saw that these two were almost exactly alike, and it was obvious that one of them had been copied. Since Mr. Newman was new to the class (he was replacing Mr. Ailing, who was sick), he did not know whether Charles Starrs, who wrote paper A, or Ulric Betcher, who wrote paper B, was the brighter and therefore the one whose paper had been copied.

Can you tell who copied whom? List the items of evidence on which you base your decision.

Solution on page 66

THE CIDER BOOTH

Farmer Isaiah, who called himself Izzy the Cider Man, had a booth at the county fair and sold cider by the glass or jug. He had nicknames for all his family and friends, and nobody knew why he invented them. His hired man, Peter Smith, was called Boody; his son Louis was called Abby; and his daughter Patricia was called Binx. And they all took turns working at the booth.

On Friday, August twelfth, the security guard at the fair (he had no name, so please give him one) saw Boody and Abby and Binx leave together, and saw Boody lock the door and then give the key to Izzy. When Izzy opened the booth the next morning, the money that should have been in the cash box was gone.

Questioned by the police, Boody said, "I always leave the money in the box—that's what Izzy told me to do. And I always look to make sure that the window is locked, and I always turn the knob to make sure that the door is locked, and I did like I always do. Abby and Binx will back me up on that, and so will Izzy." And they all did.

Who do you think took the money?

Questions

1. Had the door been forced or broken into? Yes____ No____

2. Had the shutter of the counter been forced? Yes____ No____

3. Had the screwdriver been used to force open the window? Yes____ No____

4. Had the window been forced from the outside? Yes____ No____

5. Did somebody climb through the window? Yes____ No____

6. Could Boody have climbed through the window? Yes____ No____

7. Had somebody tampered with the window lock? Yes____ No____

8. How do you think entrance was made into the booth?

9. Who stole the money?

Solution on page 66

GAMBOL

As Dr. Sinus was about to drive off to see a patient, he accidentally dropped his car keys. Picasso, the family dog, seeing a great opportunity, picked them up and scampered off, with the doctor in hot pursuit, leading to a five-minute chase around the house. The doctor, however, was out-classed, but luckily for him, just then Whiz McGonnigle came by on his bike with the idea of selling a few chances on a raffle for the benefit of the bicycle team.

Whiz, quick as usual to size up a situation, realized that if he could locate the keys, he'd end up selling quite a few raffle tickets. He studied the situation for a few moments, concentrated hard, and then went and got the keys.

Could you?

Questions

1. Did the doctor fall? Yes_____ No_____

2. Did the doctor chase Picasso? Yes_____ No_____ If so, who won?

3. Did the doctor hurt himself? Yes_____ No_____

4. Is the doctor angry at the children? Yes_____ No_____

5. Do you think the doctor was careless? Yes_____ No_____

6. Does Picasso have a mean disposition? Yes_____ No_____

7. When did Picasso get the rattle? Before taking the keys_____ While the doctor was yelling at him_____ While the doctor lay on the ground_____

8. Do you think that Whiz saw the keys from his bike? Yes_____ No_____

9. Where are the keys?

Solution on page 67

37

COOKIE JAR

The Bicker boys never got along with each other. Bonehead, who was sixteen years old, bullied Thickhead, his ten-year-old brother. They delighted in snitching on each other, with the result that their parents believed neither of them. Very often Mr. and Mrs. Bicker never did find out which one of their sons had lied, so they usually punished both of them, hoping that that would cure the boys of lying, but the practice didn't work.

When Mrs. Bicker found that $38.14 in cash was missing from the cookie jar where she'd kept it, she thought she knew who had taken it. When Bonehead accused Thickhead and pointed out the evidence, she was more certain than ever, but Mr. Bicker, who was a detective, wasn't sure. "Let's examine the evidence," he said, and they did.

Whom do you think they then accused of stealing the $38.14?

Questions

1. Bearing in mind the fact that the average kitchen counter is about three feet high, about how tall was each of the brothers? Bonehead is_____ Thickhead is_____

2. Are there any muddy footsteps other than those leading to the kitchen cabinet? Yes____ No____

3. Whose footsteps are they, judging by their size?_____

4. Whichever one it was, does it look as if he climbed onto the counter? Yes____ No____

5. Could Bonehead reach the upper shelf by standing on the floor and stretching? Yes____ No____

6. Would Thickhead have to climb onto the counter in order to reach the upper shelf? Yes____ No____

7. Do you think that the footprints were deliberately planted in order to frame one of the brothers? Yes____ No____

8. Who could have planted them?_____

9. Why do you think some bills were left on the upper shelf?

10. Who stole the $38.14?

Solution on page 68

WATER BED

Big-Lip Mosely hated dogs, children, and everybody else who didn't help him make money. And of all the children he'd ever seen, he hated the LeGrands the most, probably because they kept using a shortcut that crossed a piece of land he owned. After he'd chased them with a stick a couple of times, threatened to shoot them, and tried to get the police to arrest them, the three LeGrands (Sandra, Mickey, and Tim) decided to take appropriate counter-action.

The counter-action consisted of shinnying up a drainpipe to the porch roof, opening a window that was unlocked, and climbing into Mosely's apartment with intent to commit mischief. They separated while they looked around and did nothing worse than upsetting a few ashtrays and scrawling signs that read, "Woe unto Big-Lip!" After that they would have sneaked down the stairs to the front door, tiptoed out, and gone happily home, but one of the trio discovered the water bed. And that was irresistible.

Even so, they might have gotten away with slashing the water bed, except that the water leaked down into the apartment below, where it dripped onto the back of Mrs. Enslow's neck. After the tenth drop she called the plumber and then stood outside and waited for him. Escape for the LeGrands was thus impossible, and the plumber caught them red-handed, as you see them. Shamefacedly they had to walk downstairs where Mrs. Enslow raged and ranted and said she'd punish whoever had done the actual slashing, but luckily she wasn't smart enough to figure out who had, and they escaped before Big-Lip got home.

Can you decide who slashed the water bed?

Questions

1. Was Mosely self-important?
   Yes____ No____

2. Was he vain? Yes____ No____

3. Was he short and fat? Yes____ No____

4. Was he a dangerous man?
   Yes____ No____

5. Was he well off financially?
   Yes____ No____

6. Do you think that the water bed was punctured on purpose?
   Yes____ No____

7. Do you think that the water rushed out suddenly? Yes____ No____

8. Do you think that one of the LeGrands got soaking wet when the water bed was punctured? Yes____ No____

9. Who has wet clothes? Sandra____ Mickey____ Tim____ Nobody____

10. Who slashed the water bed?

Solution on page 69

FALSE ALARM

After Molly Pitcher Junior High had been emptied by a false alarm rung at the box which is shown, the principal, Guy High, Jr., narrowed the investigation down to the three boys who are pictured.

Bo Bo Bustum, the school bully, who was a little slow in the head, said, "Angelo did it. I saw him standing on the chair and pulling the alarm."

Claude Casement, whose father had once played in the outfield for the Cleveland Indians, said, "Angelo did it. I saw him climb up on a chair right next to the alarm. That way, he could reach the alarm. He must have done it."

Angelo Pittapat said, "I didn't even know that the alarm was there. It was my birthday and my parents took me to a concert in the afternoon. The chair? I never saw it, either."

If you were the principal, whom would you accuse of ringing the false alarm?

Questions

1. Label the footprints "A" for Angelo, "B" for Bo Bo, and "C" for Claude.

2. Was the chair moved, and if so, by whom?

3. State the order the three boys arrived in: First____ Second____ Third____

4. Do you believe Angelo's story? Yes____ No____ If you don't, why don't you?

5. Do you believe Bo Bo's story? Yes____ No____ If you don't, why don't you?

6. Do you believe Claude's story? Yes____ No____ If you don't, why don't you?

7. Describe each of the boys' gaits— whether they walked, hopped, skipped, or ran. Angelo_____ Bo Bo_____ Claude_____

8. Who set off the alarm?

Solution on page 69

WESTWARD HO-HUM!

Amos Tinkleberry was a sly old buzzard in the antique business. When he needed money, which was most of the time, he'd sell anything he had to the first person who came along at what seemed to be bargain rates. The trouble was that you could never be sure whether old Tinkleberry was selling you something genuine or something fake.

Young Kelley Fishday had ten dollars in his pocket when he walked into the Tinkleberry shop. Kelley looked around a little while, and then Tinkleberry offered him his choice of the three sketches shown here.

"Frederic Remington drew these," Tinkleberry said, speaking in a low voice, as if he were revealing a secret. "They're sketches for paintings that he did later on. Ordinarily I'd want a big price for them, but I need money and I'll take whatever I can get."

"All I have is ten dollars," Kelley said. "Is that enough?"

Tinkleberry nodded. "Sure. If it's cash."

Kelley, however, hesitated. He knew that Frederic Remington, who had died in 1909, was probably the most distinguished painter of the Old West. If Remington had really made these sketches, they were worth a lot of money. If they were fake, Kelley would be throwing away his money.

He took out his ten dollar bill and held it in his hand, and Tinkleberry stared at it as if he wanted to eat up the hand and the bill, all in one bite. "Take your choice," said Tinkleberry, speaking in a whisper. "Take any one of the three, for just ten dollars."

If you were Kelley, what would you do?

Questions

1. Would you expect the pictures to look old? Yes____ No____

2. Would you buy sketch no. 1? Yes____ No____

3. What are the reasons for your answer to question 2?

4. Would you buy sketch no. 2? Yes____ No____

5. What are your reasons for your answer to question 4?

6. Would you buy sketch no. 3? Yes____ No____

7. What are your reasons for your answer to question 6?

Solution on page 70

TRICK OR TREAT

When a small, elfin figure wearing the mask of a hobbit knocked on Shorty Flickenflacker's door and said, "Trick or treat," Flickenflacker snarled, "Trick!" and flicked the door back squarely in the boy's face, giving him a bloody nose.

The boy told his father what had happened, and his father said, "Trick? Just leave it to me. I'll show him what a trick is!"

What he did can be seen here in the sketch.

Shorty knew of three boys who were about the age and size of that small, elfin figure. Their fathers are shown here. "A" is a carpenter, "B" a major league pitcher, "C" a tennis player.

Which father played the trick on Shorty Flickenflacker?

Questions

1. What kind of liquid is in the tank?_____

2. Is the liquid clean? Yes____ No____

3. Did it require more than average strength to haul the section of oil tank to its present position? Yes____ No____

4. Which one or ones of the fathers is likely to have more than average strength? Tennis player____ Carpenter____ Pitcher____

5. Is the ladder now usable? Yes____ No____

6. Was the plank well nailed? Yes____ No____

7. Is Shorty's car inside the garage? Yes____ No____ Probably____

8. Who played the trick on Shorty?

Solution on page 71

SPELLING BEE

$\mathbf{W}$hiz McGonnigle was a shoo-in to win the county spelling championship. After all, hadn't he spelt Afghanistan, Timbuktu, and Nebuchadnezzar without a mistake, when all the other finalists had tripped up at least once? Including Marcia Hagentuckle, who had never been much of a speller until she entered into the county tournament and qualified easily. Her only mistake was when she misspelt honey, which everybody else handled with ease.

There were rumors to the effect that she was to be given the list of words ahead of time. At first Whiz refused to believe the story, but when it was pointed out that Marcia's father had a stranglehold on some of the town officials and that he'd never been known for his moral principles, Whiz got worried.

Gradually the rumors became more specific, until it was fairly certain that Marcia would be handed the list of words immediately before the actual event. As a result, Whiz made certain preparations, with the help of Kippy Ironbledder, Skinny Hobart, and a few other friends.

The sketch shows the lobby of the town hall, with the contestants and their friends waiting to be told where to go. Can you foresee what is likely to happen?

Questions

1. Do you think that Marcia is about to be given the list of words?
   Yes____ No____

2. Would Marcia have a chance to read such a list? Yes____ No____

3. Does the man signalling to Marcia have a suspicious list of words?
   Yes____ No____

4. If he tripped or fell, would someone have a chance to grab his list?
   Yes____ No____

5. Could the list be made useless by some physical means? Yes____ No____

6. If something occurred to create general confusion, could the list then be taken?
   Yes____ No____

7. Name at least seven things calculated to create confusion and thus ruin the Hagentuckle conspiracy.

8. What do you think happened?

Solution on page 71

THE GREAT DIAMOND HEIST

Whiz McGonnigle was no athlete, but he could ride a mean bike. That was why his mother had asked him to go to the butcher's and pick up the steak she'd ordered. On the way back Whiz heard the sound of a crash, and also heard one of the drivers, Mrs. Minnie Rahrah (she was a great football fan), scream out that she'd lost her million-dollar diamond.

"I was wearing it on a chain around my neck," Mrs. Rahrah moaned. "I don't know what happened to it. Find it for me. Oh, my!"

A two-man police cruiser had reached the scene immediately before Whiz and his bike. While one cop was still examining Minnie to make sure she was still in one piece, the second cop was questioning the driver of the other car. Neither he nor the other police officer who came shortly afterwards and examined the immediate area were able to find the diamond or any trace of it.

Whiz, however, listened carefully to the questioning of the driver of the other car, then jumped on his bike and pedaled off.

Can you tell how he knew where to go, and why he went there?

Questions

1. Did the driver of the small car block the road on purpose? Yes_____ No_____

2. Was he in the car at the time of the accident? Yes_____ No_____

3. Would the police ask him to identify himself? Yes_____ No_____

4. Do you think that Minnie was driving fast? Yes_____ No_____

5. Did she try to avoid the accident? Yes_____ No_____

6. Do you think that she lost consciousness? Yes_____ No_____

7. Was the diamond stolen? Yes_____ No_____

8. Was the dog on a leash at any time? Yes_____ No_____

9. Did the dog run away before the accident? Yes_____ No_____

10. What was Whiz waiting for?

11. Did he recover the diamond, and if so, how?

Solution on page 72

THE GENTLE BREEZES

Whiz McGonnigle and Kippy Ironbledder were counting out the money they'd collected for the new hockey rink, when the phone rang and they both jumped up and ran into the house. When they got back a few minutes later, fifty-five dollars in bills were gone.

With the help of a ladder, Kippy got to the top of the wall and recognized Ruddy Newsome, who was sitting on the grass further down the empty lane. When Ruddy saw Kippy, Ruddy jumped up and started to run off, although limping badly. Since Kippy knew that there was usually a police car parked on the main road, he yelled. As a result, the police stopped Ruddy, searched him, and found fifty-five dollars.

"It blew over the wall," Ruddy said, "so I picked it up. Whiz and Kippy admit they left the bills on the table, don't they? So what's wrong with picking up a few bills when I don't know where they came from? And tell me—how could I climb a wall as high as that one?"

The police scratched their heads and had no answer. "Better go inside McGonnigles' house and get that leg of yours fixed up," they said. In the yard Ruddy repeated the answer he'd given to the police, but Whiz and Kippy didn't believe him. Why not?

Questions

1. Was there a brisk wind blowing?
   Yes_____ No_____

2. Could a wind blow bills over the wall?
   Yes_____ No_____

3. Could Ruddy see the money while he was walking next to the wall?
   Yes_____ No_____

4. Do you think Ruddy could have climbed the wall without aid of some sort? Yes_____ No_____

5. Was there a way of scaling the wall?
   Yes_____ No_____

6. Can you disprove Ruddy's story?
   Yes_____ No_____

7. Do you think Ruddy stole the money?
   Yes_____ No_____ If your answer is yes, explain how.

Solution on page 73

IDORA PARK

One day early in the spring the McGonnigles went to Idora Amusement Park. The senior McGonnigles wisely turned Whiz and Martha loose. "Meet us at the flagpole in two hours," they were told, "and enjoy yourselves."

The young McGonnigles did, but at the very beginning of their morning they had an adventure. They were walking on Main Street and had just passed The Emporium when they saw a man in a green-striped shirt run out of the store and yell something that no one understood. About five seconds later (time it, see how long five seconds is and how far you can run in that time) a guard came rushing out of the The Emporium and pointed at the man in the green-striped shirt. "Stop him!" the guard called out. "He's a thief—he stole some watches—stop him!"

Another guard further up the street did stop him. The man in the green-striped shirt said, "It's all a mistake—I didn't take anything—search me." Which the second guard did, and found nothing.

Meanwhile the first guard questioned several witnesses. They all agreed that the thief had had a small package and had disposed of it somewhere.

"He dropped it in the street-cleaner's can," the first witness said. *"I saw him!"*

"He dropped it in the mouth of that tuba," the second witness said. *"I saw him!"*

"He dropped it in the wheelchair lady's lap," the third witness said. *"I saw him!"*

The guard scratched his head and frowned, because all he found in the tuba and can and wheelchair were little packages filled with shredded newspapers. Neither Whiz nor Martha did any scratching. They didn't have to, because they agreed on where the watches were and who had them. Do you know?

Questions

1. Do you think that the three witnesses lied? Yes____ No____

2. Are the three places mentioned by the witnesses reasonable ways of getting rid of the loot? Yes____ No____

3. Do you think that the thief had an accomplice? Yes____ No____ Probably____

4. Do you think that the thief deliberately brought attention to himself? Yes____ No____

5. Do you think that the "drops" were parts of a scheme to confuse people? Yes____ No____

6. Can you find any place other than the can, the tuba, or the lady's lap where the thief could have disposed of his loot? Yes____ No____

7. Who had the loot?_____

Solution on page 74

THE BIG BANG

Whiz McGonnigle tried out for a part in a school play and was turned down. He was no actor. He was almost home on the school bus and about to get off, when through the window he saw somebody in a red jacket fiddling with the padlock of the shed where he kept his new, fifteen-speed bicycle that Minnie Rahrah had given him. Whiz knew he had locked the shed before he went to school that morning.

The man seemed to be having trouble with the padlock, but when Whiz jumped off the bus and yelled (he shouldn't have), the man got on a bike that was lying in the high grass and rode off. Whiz was almost positive that it was *his* new bike. Angry and excited, he ran to the house and shouted out the news of the theft.

Mr. McGonnigle called the police at once, who rounded up four men with red jackets and called back and asked Whiz to come to the police station to identify the thief. Whiz had been too far away for that, but he kept wondering why the thief had had so much trouble with the padlock.

Before going to the police station with his father and Martha, Whiz gave Martha a balloon. "Blow it up," he said, "and stick a pin in it when I scratch my nose at the police station."

The sketch shows the scene at the police station a moment after the loud bang when Martha did her balloon act. Whiz, overjoyed that his idea had worked, pointed to one of the men and said, "Him. He's the thief."

Whom did he point out and why?

Questions

1. Do you think that the thief had unlocked the shed? Yes____ No____

2. Did all the men turn instinctively at the bang of the burst balloon? Yes____ No____

3. Do you think that the thief would look guilty? Yes____ No____

4. Can you see anything different in the glances of the three men? Yes____ No____

5. Would a one-eyed person have trouble with the lock? Yes____ No____

6. Was it important for the thief to relock the shed? Yes____ No____

7. Which of the four men stole the bike?

Solution on page 74

SOLUTIONS

Solution to *Bomb Sight* (p. 10)

1. Yes. It has explosive material, a battery to create a spark, and a device for connecting the battery.

2. Yes. You bet it is, no matter what kind of a bomb.

3. Yes.

4. Yes, although bombs are tricky, and handling them is a very dangerous job that should be left to a police bomb squad.

5. Yes.

6. The wires from the battery are connected to themselves and are therefore incapable of exploding the bomb, regardless of whether the clock mechanism works.

7. What Whiz actually said was, "Bum bomb." Any answer showing that he knew the bomb to be harmless is correct.

Solution to *Watch Out!* (p. 12)

1. (1) In A the watch is on the night table, but in B it is in the armchair, where you can barely see it.
(2) In A the junk candy is on the bureau, but in B it is in the armchair.
(3) In A there are almonds in the dish on the night table, but in B they are in the armchair.
(4) In B the edge of the rug is torn, but it's not in A.
(5) In B the clock shows 1:55, but in A it is 11:10.

(6) In B the box of tissues is torn, but it's not in A.
(7) In B the box of matches has been spilled on the floor, but in A the box is on the bureau.
(8) In B the eyeglasses are on the floor, but in A they're on the bureau.
(9) In B the pitcher of water is full, but in A it's only a third full.
(10) In B the window curtains are hanging straight, but in A one of them is crooked.

2. Yes, because the pitcher has been filled and the curtain has been straightened up.

3. No, because the money is still on the bureau in B. A thief would have taken it.

4. All the evidence points to a pack rat. The manner in which various objects have been taken and placed in a kind of hiding place in the armchair indicates the habits of a pack rat, and his hole can be seen in the baseboard next to the bureau. Furthermore, all the objects removed indicate the work of a small rodent, who wouldn't be strong enough to move a clock or a water pitcher.

pack rat

Solution to *Made in Japan* (p. 14)

1. Next to the pile of presents, where she's standing now.

2. With water from the pitcher. The pitcher, since it does not match the rest of the china and since there are no glasses on the table, was probably brought from the kitchen in order to put out the fire.

3. Yes, judging by the chairs that have been knocked over and by the general air of confusion.

4. Because it was dark, and because everyone was busy putting out the fire.

5. Yes. The thief smeared the frosting while reaching out for the netsuke, and also stained the tablecloth with jelly from the edge of the cake.

6. In the chair facing the jelly stain and the smeared frosting.

7. The girl who is licking her wrist, which must have gotten frosting on it, as pointed out in the answer to question 5.

netsuke

Solution to *Buried Gold* (p. 16)

1. Yes, that's a fair guess, particularly because there is punctuation.

2. Yes.

3. Cellar corner, two feet from end, four feet up, move broken brick.

4. Exactly where the secret message indicated, which is where Wendy found the gold.

Solution to *Stolen Bases* (p. 18)

1. The first baseman is wearing a catcher's mask.

2. The catcher is wearing swimming fins.

3. Home plate is backwards.

4. There are unequal distances between the bases.

5. The runner between second and third base is hopping on one foot in the wrong direction.

6. The pitcher is standing in front of the rubber, instead of on or behind it.

7. There is no batter's box.

8. The foul lines are wobbly.

9. The bags are outside the foul line.

10. There are four outfielders, making ten men on the team.
    Note that there is nothing wrong in having four outfielders, provided the total team has nine players. You can place your nine men wherever you want.

Solution to *Picnic* (p. 20)

1. Yes, judging by the expensive clothes and beach equipment.

2. Yes. That's one of the characteristics that marks them as expensive.

3. Yes.

4. Yes.

5. No. The teacher and the chauffeur are

near Gwendolyn's things and would surely have noticed anyone meddling.

6. No. She was too fond of her new watch to have taken it into the water.

7. Crows are notorious for being attracted by shiny objects, and it is highly likely that a crow picked up the watch and flew off with it. The likelihood is increased by the presence of the crows, of bird tracks near Gwendolyn's clothes, and of a crow's nest in the tree.

When Whiz told his parents about it, they called the police and told them Whiz's theory. The next day a policeman climbed the tree with the crow's nest. The resident crow became highly excited at this invasion of his privacy, and just before the cop reached the nest, the crow flew off with the watch in his beak. About a hundred yards out over the ocean, he let it drop. Whether it was really waterproof, nobody has ever discovered.

Solution to *Piggy Bank* (p. 22)

1. Yes.

2. Yes. A beard is one of the most common of all disguises.

3. Yes.

4. Yes. Don't you look a lot different after you've had your hair cut?

5. Yes, but highly unlikely. Plastic surgery is expensive.

6. They all do.

7. B's is closest.

8. C's ears are most like Hardy's.

9. C—the identification depends on similarity of ears, because ears are the one feature that it is almost impossible to change. Nevertheless Hard-Hearted Hardy insisted on his innocence. "Those kids," he said, "never even looked at my ears. I know, because I was there."

Solution to *Blot it Out* (p. 24)

1. Whiz and Skinny found a dusty old mirror, held the blotter up to it, and read it in the reflection, which you can do, too. The letter said:

Dear Joe,
These people I'm working for, the Ho-
barts, are really loaded. They have the
kind of safe you won't have much trou-
ble with, hidden behind a picture of
some cows. So next Wednesday after-
noon, when the Hobarts go to a concert,
nobody's home except that kid of theirs,
but we can take care of him. Just bring
along a bottle of chloroform—or even
better than that, I can make him have a
little accident, say a broken leg. He goes
up to the attic all the time, and that's
where I'll make it happen.

All my love, from
your sweetheart Cheri

After deciphering the letter, the best thing for Whiz and Skinny to do is bolt the attic door and put furniture and trunks and heavy stuff against it, and then try to attract attention from the outside—by a window, if possible. Otherwise they'll have to wait it out until the Hobarts return.

Which the boys did. By that time Joe and Cheri had run off, and when Skinny told his father what had happened and showed him the blotter, Mr. Hobart called the police.

As for Mrs. Hobart, she gave Skinny a big hug and then she sighed. "Oh," she said. "Cheri was such a good cook!"

Solution to *Seeing Double* (p. 26)

There are almost too many differences to count here, but the most important ones are:

1. "A" shows only one cloud, while "B" shows several and the artist has used her imagination in drawing them. One almost looks like a cat.

2. "A" shows four windows on the house, and their details, but "B" shows only two windows and doesn't show their details.

3. "A" shows the shingles on the roof and "B" doesn't.

4. "A" shows several cars, but "B" shows only one car.

5. "A" shows a road sign, but "B" doesn't.

6. "A" shows several people playing ball,

but "B" shows only one player.

7. "A" shows shadows, but "B" doesn't.

8. "A" shows a butterfly, but "B" doesn't.

9. "A" shows smoke coming from the chimney, but "B" doesn't.

10. "A" shows the details of the trees and

flowers, but "B" doesn't.

11. "A" shows a television antenna, but "B" doesn't.

12. "A" shows the birds very clearly in the sky, but "B" shows them only as smudges.

Lily, who may become a scientist when she grows up, tried to show absolutely everything that was in front of her. She doesn't have the skill to show all of the details properly, and there are too many of them for her to have included every one in the drawing, but she did the best that she could.

Violet, on the other hand, drew her picture in a general way, rather than focussing on exact details. She is more concerned with the "impression" that an object gives than with exactness. While this difference in their personalities is interesting, the main point of this puzzle is this: if you remember that people tend to see things differently based on their own interests and experiences, it will help you when you listen to witnesses describe what they have seen. Keep in mind that while different people will describe the same scene in completely different ways, and each of them will think that he or she is being absolutely accurate, there is no such thing as complete accuracy of observation.

Solution to *International Crisis* (p. 28)

1. Poison. With the embassy alerted, it would be difficult to reach the conference room carrying a knife, gun, or bomb without being noticed.

2. No, because he or she would be under the observation of the other delegates, particularly if they knew of the threat.

3. Yes.

4. Yes. As a waiter he would have an excellent opportunity for putting poison in some of the food.

5. The chocolates, particularly the one with a nut on it, because the nut could be lifted up, a poison capsule inserted, and the nut then replaced.

6. Yes. All the dishes are well filled ex-

cept the dish of chocolate, which has only three pieces, probably to guarantee that all would be eaten, including the fatal one.

7. No, but she could make a pretty good guess.

8. She grabbed what she thought was the poisonous chocolate. The waiter, who was really the terrorist in disguise, could do nothing about it, and watched in dismay while Martha went over to her father, showed him the chocolate, and told him of her suspicions. With that, the terrorist turned around and walked out of the room, but he was caught by the embassy security guards, who had been alerted by Martha's father.

The delegates, when they learned what had happened, were afraid to eat anything lest it, too, be poisoned. They therefore signed the treaty as soon as possible, and they all went without dinner. But Martha knew all the chefs and they assured her that everything else was safe. Consequently she gorged herself and had a stomachache next morning.

Solution to *Picture Gallery* (p. 30)

1. Yes. There are hundreds of examples of fooling the public.

2. Not with absolute certainty. Controversy still rages over some paintings which experts have studied to the best of their ability without being able to ascertain their authenticity.

3. Probably, as pointed out in answer 2. Experts can usually spot copies, but not always.

4. No. The canvas has rotted on many works of art, either because of age or the poor quality of the medium painted on, and a technique has been developed for placing the painting face down, removing the old canvas without hurting the painting, and then pasting a new canvas onto the back. Then presto! You have an old painting on new canvas.

5. Yes. These methods are commonly used to give sure proof of the age of a painting.

6. The still life of the flowers, which casts the same shadow as all the paintings in A. On the second visit Whiz noted that all the paintings with one exception cast shadows different from what he'd seen the first time. He concluded that he was seeing a painting of a painting, and that it had been copied with the shadow as it existed in A. The thief removed the real painting, pasted the painting of the painting in its place, and nobody noticed the difference until Whiz pointed it out.

The kind of painting that looks so real

that it fools you is called *trompe l'oeil,* which is French and means "fools the eye." It goes back thousands of years ago to the legend of the Greek painter who painted grapes so realistically that birds came and pecked at them.

In the nineteenth century it was fashionable for wealthy people to have someone paint these *trompe l'oeil* paintings on their walls, so that it looked as if there were a lake or a beautiful garden outside. Sometimes they just had a door painted, but the fashion has disappeared, maybe because *trompe l'oeil* is so hard to pronounce—except, of course, for a Frenchman.

Solution to *The Cheater* (p. 32)

1. A wrote without stopping, whereas B stopped in the middle of several words, as if he had to have another look at what he was copying.

2. A inked out some words, as if he had a better idea, whereas B copied the words he saw and didn't change his mind because he didn't have much of a mind to begin with.

3. An outstanding difference between the papers comes at the very end, as if A had gotten up and handed in his paper before B had a chance to copy the last few words, which B then misspelt.

4. B's writing was smaller than A's and should have had more words to the line, but in copying A's paper exactly, B used the same number of words per line, although a different spacing would have been more natural for him and would have filled the page better.

Conclusion: U. Betcher, who wrote paper B, copied C. Starrs's test.

Solution to *The Cider Booth* (p. 34)

1. No, there are no marks on the door that indicate a forcible entry.

2. No, there are no marks on it, either, and the padlock looks secure.

3. Yes, because the imperfections of the screwdriver match the marks on the windowsill.

4. No, the tool marks indicate that the window was forced from the inside.

5. Yes, because a shred of cloth was

caught, and because somebody must have climbed in. How else could the money have been stolen?

6. No, he was too fat.

7. Yes, judging by the loose screw.

8. Somebody climbed in through the window and his or her clothing caught on a nail and left a shred of cloth. Since the lock was loose and not operating, all the person had to do was slide up the window, climb in, and, after the theft, put the lock loosely in place, climb out, and lower the window.

9. Binx. Although shabbily dressed, she has a new and expensive hairdo, manicured fingernails, and a new piece of jewelry; all of which cost a lot of money. It follows that she probably stole it from the cash box. She must have unscrewed the lock during the afternoon. Boody merely glanced at the lock and thought it was securely fastened.

After Binx had climbed in and stolen the money, she faked the tool marks on the windowsill and left the screwdriver where it would be found easily and would be assumed to have been used to force the window. But by mistake she put the tool marks on the inside instead of on the outside part of the windowsill.

She also has a patch on her jeans, which means she might have caught them on the nail. After having been questioned by the police, she confessed and burst into tears, thus ruining her new make-up.

Solution to *Gambol* (p. 36)

1. Yes, judging by the dirt and mussiness of his clothes, the rip in his pants, and the marks on the dirt at the right.

2. Yes, and Picasso won big. After all, he took the keys.

3. Yes. He scratched his cheek.

4. Yes, and with a vengeance, because they left a rope in the yard that he tripped over.

5. Yes, first in dropping his keys, and second in not watching his step and thus tripping over the rope.

6. No, he's just having fun. In his world, keys are to play with.

7. Probably while the doctor lay on the ground. Otherwise the doctor would have seen Picasso drop the keys, which he no longer has, and would know where they are.

8. No, they are nowhere in sight. If we can't see them, how can he?

9. Hidden by the toys in the playpen. It is obvious that the dog must have dropped the keys in order to pick up the rattle, and the playpen is the most

likely place to have made the exchange.

Whiz picked up the keys and handed them politely to the doctor, together with the raffle book that Whiz had come to sell. The doctor, however, threw down the raffle book and took the keys.

Moral: You can't sell anything to an angry man.

Solution to *Cookie Jar* (p. 38)

1. Bonehead is about six feet tall, and Thickhead is about four and a half to five feet tall.

2. Yes. There are the ones behind Thickhead.

3. Thickhead's.

4. Yes.

5. Yes, barely so. The upper shelf is about six and a half feet high, and Bonehead is six feet. He could just about reach it.

6. Yes, obviously. He's too short to reach from the floor.

7. Yes, because they reach the counter and then do not appear again, as if somebody had planted them by hand and then left.

8. Bonehead could have planted them, but Thickhead could also have done so, and then claimed that Bonehead was trying to frame him.

9. Because Bonehead would have had to stretch and thus would use only one arm and would feel for the jar, but would not see the bills. Thickhead, however, if he stood on the counter, would see the bills and would certainly have taken them.

10. Bonehead, for the reasons given in answer 9.

    When Thickhead grew up and was the same size as his brother, he hit Bonehead with a baseball bat and sent him to the hospital for two months. As a result, Thickhead was sentenced to five years in prison for assault and attempted murder.

    When Bonehead recovered, he applied for and got a job as a prison guard, where he bullied Thickhead and tried to kill him. The result of *that* was that Bonehead was sentenced to the same prison, where the brothers are now cellmates.

Solution to *Water Bed* (p. 40)

1. Yes, judging by the certificates and phony medals on the walls of his bedroom.

2. Yes, judging by all the pictures of himself.

3. Yes, according to the pictures.

4. Yes. He had a collection of weapons and had threatened to shoot the LeGrand children.

5. Yes. He had good furniture and plenty of clothes.

6. Yes, judging by the gash and by the sabre on the bed.

7. Yes. The pressure inside would make it rush out fast.

8. Yes, because the water must have gushed out suddenly, and whoever did the puncturing would be soaking wet.

9. Nobody.

10. Sandra, because she's wearing Big-Lip's slacks, which are much too big for her, and which she exchanged for her own wet slacks. The pleats show that she must have taken a tuck in the waistband, probably with a safety pin. Mosely's slacks could be the right length for her, but his waist was far bigger than hers, and his dry clothes were easy to take from the open closet.

    Having solved the problem of dry clothes, she still had to get rid of her wet ones, which she did by shoving them down the laundry chute. In due time the laundry was brought up to Big-Lip, who put his clothes away without even looking at them.

    As for Sandra, she wondered what to do with Big-Lip's slacks, which she didn't like and didn't want. She solved *that* problem, however, by giving them to the local thrift shop, where Big-Lip bought them about six months later. He found that they fit him perfectly, and he thought he had a bargain.

Solution to *False Alarm* (p. 42)

1. Angelo's footprints are the small ones, Bo Bo's are those of the worn sneakers, and Claude's are those of the running shoes.

2. Yes. The track of the chair shows clearly that it was pushed from the lower part of the picture to its present position by Bo Bo.

3. Angelo, then Bo Bo, then Claude. This can be figured out because Bo Bo's footprints indicate that he shoved the chair up to the wall. Claude came later

69

because his footprints circle the chair and are superimposed on Bo Bo's. Angelo came before Bo Bo because Angelo's path is broken where the chair must have been before Bo Bo moved it. Angelo climbed onto the chair and then jumped from it before it was moved under the alarm.

4. No. Angelo lied about not having seen the chair, on the seat of which his footprints are imprinted, because the evidence shows he jumped from the chair, as indicated in answer 3.

5. No. Bo Bo lied about seeing Angelo at the alarm, because Angelo had already left by the time Bo Bo arrived.

6. No. Claude lied in saying he saw Angelo climb onto the chair, because the evidence shows that Angelo climbed onto the chair before it was near the alarm, and Angelo's footprints are nowhere near the alarm.

7. Angelo walked, then climbed the chair, then jumped from it and resumed walking. Bo Bo walked. Claude walked as far as the alarm, circled the chair, and then ran, which you can tell because only his toe-prints show after he circled the chair.

8. Claude. He is so tall that he could have easily reached the alarm even though the chair was in front of it, and his running away from it is suspicious. Besides, he was the last one to approach the alarm.

Solution to *Westward Ho-Hum!* (p. 44)

1. No. Old sketches on good paper do not necessarily look old or faded.

2. No.

3. There is an aerial on one of the houses, which is anachronistic*. Furthermore, American Indians have straight hair, and one of the Indians has curly hair. So this is not a real Remington.

4. No.

5. One of the galloping horses has all four feet on the ground, which is incorrect. A painter of Remington's knowledge would never make such a mistake. Also, the American flag in this picture has fifty stars. In 1909, when Remington died, there were only forty-six states, and the flag had only forty-six stars. So this sketch contains an anach-

---

* An anachronism is something that could not exist at the time that is indicated. For example, if a book about Christopher Columbus had a picture in it that showed him setting out to discover America in an airplane, the picture would be an anachronism because airplanes didn't exist in Columbus's day.

ronism too, and isn't a real Remington.

6. No.

7. The Indians are wearing running

shoes—another anachronism, because shoes like this didn't exist in 1909. This sketch is also a fake.

Solution to *Trick or Treat* (p. 46)

1. Oil, judging by the trail of spilt liquid from the tank to the oil container.

2. No. The oil is dark and obviously dirty, and is probably old engine oil, which is worthless and easy to get.

3. Yes. The oil tank is heavy.

4. All three.

5. No. It's slippery and will smear whatever touches it.

6. No, this is a botched job, with bent nails.

7. Probably. It's not likely that anyone would lock an empty garage, particularly because unlocking the padlock would be a nuisance.

8. The tennis player. His left forearm is overdeveloped, indicating he is left-handed, whereas the pitcher's right forearm is overdeveloped, indicating he is right-handed. The angle of the bent nails indicates a hammer swung with the left hand. As for the carpenter, he would do a far neater job.

Solution to *Spelling Bee* (p. 48)

1. Yes. She is looking at a man who seems to be signalling to her.

2. Yes. It is apparently permissible to do some last-minute reading before entering the main hall.

3. Yes.

4. Yes.

5. Yes. If the list was smeared with paint or glue, Marcia couldn't hold it without virtually confessing what she'd done.

6. Yes.

7. One student has a white rat which she can let loose; another has a whistle; another has a water pistol, another has a sling-shot; another is ready to pull

down a trophy; another is poised to pour out a pot of glue; two others hold a wire and are ready to trip up the man with the list.

8. At a given signal, the seven plans were set in motion, and all heck broke loose. In the confusion, Skinny grabbed the list, although he showed it to no one, least of all to Whiz.

After the Hagentuckle conspiracy failed, Marcia defaulted and Whiz went on to win by spelling the word "phantasmagoria." When he was being awarded the prize, he said, "I know what the word means, too."

He should never have said that, because the MC said, "Good. Then define it for us."

Whiz stammered and blushed, and all of a sudden he couldn't talk. He knew what the word meant, but defining it was something else again. You see, he was no lexicographer.

Still, he had the silver cup, and he'd won it fairly.

Solution to *The Great Diamond Heist* (p. 50)

1. Yes. According to his tire marks, he parked at right angles to the direction of the road, thus blocking it.

2. No, judging by his footprints, which wander around the area rather than going directly to the other car, and by the fact that he wasn't hurt.

3. Yes, most certainly.

4. Yes, judging by the fact that she skidded, and by the considerable length of her skid marks.

5. Yes. The skid marks show that she jammed on her brakes.

6. Yes. Otherwise she would have held on to her necklace and nobody could have taken it.

7. Yes, as shown in answer 6.

8. Yes, where the dog's prints are parallel to the prints that belong to the driver of the small car.

9. No. His paw prints are on top of Minnie's tire marks, which means that he ran off after the accident.

10. For the dog to return to its home.

11. Yes. Since the diamond had disappeared and the police could neither find it nor prove who'd taken it, the dog was the only answer left. It seemed certain that the man had planned the accident in order to steal the diamond during the resulting confusion. Since he knew he might be searched, he brought his dog with him and gave the dog the diamond.

Whiz figured this out, and realized that the dog must have been trained to take objects to its home, which is where Whiz went after hearing the thief give his address to the police. Knowing that the dog would probably have the diamond in its mouth and that it would not give it up to a stranger like Whiz, he offered it the steak. Obviously the dog took the steak and Whiz took the diamond, which he brought home.

When he told his parents what had happened, they were proud of him and didn't blame him for leaving them meatless. In fact, they laughed about it and they all went out to a restaurant where they had shish-kebobs. The next day Whiz returned the diamond to Minnie. She said he was a smart little boy and she wanted to give him something. When she asked him what he'd like, Whiz said he'd love to have a new fifteen-speed bicycle. Mrs. Rahrah gulped and wrote out a check.

Solution to *The Gentle Breezes* (p. 52)

1. Yes, judging by the swirl of leaves.

2. Yes.

3. No, but he could see it while on the road at the top of the hill.

4. No.

5. Yes. With the help of a ladder, it would be easy.

6. Yes. Birds always face into the wind (because if they don't, the wind ruffles up their feathers), and here they are facing to the right. Therefore the wind was blowing to the left, away from the lane, and the bills could not have been blown over the wall.

7. Yes. He lied about the wind blowing the money over the wall, he lied about not knowing where the bills came from, and he lied about being unable to get to the top of the wall.

Actually, while on the hill he saw Whiz and Kippy counting money inside the garden. When Ruddy reached the garden wall, the ladder was lying on the outside. He propped it against the wall, climbed to the top, dropped the ladder on the garden side, and jumped down and took the money. Then, with the help of the ladder, he remounted the wall, pushed the ladder back into the garden, and jumped down into the lane. He apparently hurt his ankle on the second jump and was nursing it when Kippy saw him.

Ruddy, faced with the proof that he'd lied about the wind blowing the money over the wall, confessed. "I don't play hockey," he said, "so why wouldn't I take the money?"

Solution to *Idora Park* (p. 54)

1. No. They would have no reason to lie.

2. Yes.

3. Probably, because he didn't have the loot when, at his own request, the second guard searched him.

4. Yes. He came out yelling, whereas a thief usually wants quite the opposite—not to be noticed.

5. Yes, because he dropped packages in plain sight.

6. Yes. The small boy sitting on the curb is holding his hat upside down, and someone could easily drop a small package into it.

7. The small boy with the funny hat is the accomplice, and the loot is in his hat.

Solution to *The Big Bang* (p. 56)

1. Yes. Whiz had locked it, and yet the thief has the bicycle. He therefore must have opened the lock.

2. Yes. Wouldn't you?

3. No, not if he was a professional. Professional thieves specialize in not looking guilty.

4. Yes. One man has turned only one eye towards the sound, indicating that he probably has a glass eye.

5. Yes. A person with only one eye would have trouble with spatial relationships and would find it difficult to put the bar into its slot. To show this one-eyed difficulty, close one eye, spread your arms, and then, with one-eyed vision, try to bring your two forefingers so that their tips touch. With two eyes it's easy to do, but with one eye it isn't.

6. Yes. The unlocked shed would probably be noticed at once, whereas the locked shed would not, and would give the thief time to cover his tracks.

7. The man with the glass eye, for reasons expressed above.

WHAT THE YOUNG DETECTIVE OUGHT TO KNOW

A young detective has to learn many things, such as how to use *all* his senses—sight, hearing, touch, taste, smell—and how to interpret what he has experienced.

The well-trained detective also has to learn a great deal about criminal law. He has to know when he can arrest somebody, what the rights of a suspect are, and when a policeman has the right to shoot (which he has only if his own life is in danger or if he sees somebody actually committing a serious crime and trying to run away). A good officer knows that his real job is to prevent crime, arrest only when necessary, and keep a cool head.

Observation and the ability to ask questions (interrogation) are the most important assets of a good detective. If he's looking at a room hoping to find some clues, he uses what is called the grid method. After a general study of the room, he looks along an imaginary path about three feet wide. He starts at the ceiling, lets his eyes slide down the wall to the floor, and then looks along the floor to where he's standing, searching for clues every second. After he's covered one side of the room in this way, he goes to a wall at right angles and does the same thing. Thus the imaginary paths cross each other and would, if sketched, look like a gridiron. That's why it's called the grid method.

A trained detective never questions a suspect in the presence of other people, except other policemen or officials, because anyone within earshot (such as another suspect) might learn things that he didn't know before.

 Unless there is already a strong light, the detective will use "oblique" light (shining a flashlight at an angle) to find small objects, because the beam will cast shadows that show objects of different shape or color, such as hair, fragments of bullets, or bloodstains.

Sometimes you need a fingerprint to examine or compare with other prints, and either it's in an awkward place or else it's on a large object, like a bureau. Place a piece of scotch tape over the fingerprint, press down and then peel off the scotch tape. You'll find that it has lifted the fingerprint.

Examining fingerprints is highly technical, and most people think that the expert dusts a surface, brings out a fingerprint, and presto!—he knows who has committed the crime.

It isn't like that at all. In the first place, if the surface is rough or wet, you won't find a print. That's why, despite what you've seen on TV or read in some stories, it's almost impossible to find a print on the stock (handle) of a pistol or revolver, which is rough. Add hands that are sweaty from nervousness, and fingers that are sliding or moving, and you will realize that police usually find smudges rather than good, clear prints. But when they do find a good print, watch out!

There are expert photographers in every police department, but a good detective often makes a quick sketch of the scene of the crime, mostly to show where various objects are and where the crime was committed. He doesn't have to be an artist to do this. He simply draws shapes and jots down a word or two so that he can remember the scene accurately, long after the crime has been committed.

A detective marks every piece of evidence, either by tying a tag around it or scratching his initials on it, or both. His purpose is to be able to swear in court, if necessary, that this particular screwdriver, and not another, similar one, was found at the scene.

The work of the police artist is often important in identifying a criminal. A witness may have seen him, but a verbal description is usually of little help. Try, for instance, to describe someone you know well and then ask somebody to draw

a picture based on what you've said. It probably won't look much like the subject. That's why the police artist shows the witness a number of pictures and says, "Was his nose like this one? Or like this one, or this?" And so on, until the artist has a fair idea of the kind of nose he should draw.

He then proceeds in a similar way with other features, such as eyes, mouth, chin, shape of face, kind of hair, hairline, ears, and so on. The artist then makes a drawing based on what the witness has selected. (You've seen drawings like this in the newspapers.) If both witness and artist have done their jobs well, the witness will know that the sketch is a reasonable likeness of the suspect.

Also, a good detective will memorize not only the portrait of a person, but the way the person moves and speaks, his accent and gestures, his small, individual peculiarities, many of which he isn't even aware of himself, like the way he rubs his nose or talks out of the side of his mouth.

The qualities of a good detective—being able to observe well and keep a cool head—are not only useful in detecting crime, but will help you in whatever you do—for instance, sports, acting, science, or art.

Congratulations!

Now that you've completed all the puzzles in
You're the Detective, you qualify as a card-
carrying member of the Lawrence Treat Number
One Sleuth Club.

No. 1 Sleuth

_____

is a member in good standing of the
Lawrence Treat Number One Sleuth Club

_____   _____
(sleuth's signature)   (date)

By Lawrence Treat:

CRIME AND PUZZLEMENT: *24 Solve-Them-Yourself Picture Mysteries*, illustrated by Leslie Cabarga, $7.95.

CRIME AND PUZZLEMENT 2: *24 More Solve-Them-Yourself Picture Mysteries*, illustrated by Kathleen Borowik, $7.95.

CRIME AND PUZZLEMENT 3: *24 Solve-Them-Yourself Picture Mysteries*, illustrated by Paul Karasik, $7.95.